King of Alphas

Alisha Fiuza

DEDICATION

To all those who stayed

1. COMPETITION

Rosalyn and I stepped out of the cab, arriving at the school where my archery competition was taking place. Students roam outside, some on their lunch breaks it seemed or skipping class.

I open the trunk grabbing everything I need before we make our way inside. The high school is quite large, three floors to be exact. The gym was big enough to hold the competition.

When we enter the school, we make our way to the gym, following the directions on the walls to get there.

Rose huffs out a breath. "This place is like a maze, we're already lost."

I laugh at Rose. "I'm just following the directions."

"Well can we hurry because I need to pee. Really badly. And by the size of this place, I'm going to need a freaking GPS to find the washroom."

I roll my eyes. "You have the smallest bladder in the world."

Rose gives me a pointed look. "You think I don't already know that? I barely drank any water on the way here."

I smile when we reach the gym and when we enter, I'm met with a sign in table. Many archers are already here, prepping and I feel nerves settle in the pit of my gut. I sign in and as I walk further into the gym, bleachers fill with students. Targets line the one wall at the far end, varying in size. On the other side is where all the archers are. Pieces of paper with our last names are taped to the wall letting us know where we can set up. Once I find the word Kennedy, Rose takes off to the washroom quickly while I set up.

I take out my black recurve bow, running my hands along its smooth surface. I set it down and I move to my quiver filling it with my arrows.

Rose returns with a smile on her face. "So you ready?"

I look around at the other archers around me, most of the adults. I'm the youngest one here. "I'd be lying if I said I wasn't feeling intimidated right now."

Rose looks around, sizing up the competition. "You're the best archer I know, you got this. Now turn around, I'll tie up your hair."

I scrunch up my eyebrows. "I'm the only archer you know."

Rose completely ignores what I say by pulling half of my burgundy hair up and braiding it. The other half of my straight hair rests on my shoulders.

From where I sit, more and more students fill in empty seats on the bleachers. A group of guys catch my attention as they walk into the gym. One looks strange—but not in a bad way—like a puzzle I need to figure out.

He has black hair as dark as the night and deep blue eyes like an ocean. He has a nice square jawline and I can't help but imagine my fingers tracing the way his jaw curves. He looks over six feet tall and his black shirt defines his toned body.

The rest of his group walk behind him, ignoring the number of girls gawking at them.

I snort, must be a regular at this school.

Their eyes roam across the room as if looking for something, but then the man's eyes land on me and I feel like my heart has stopped.

Sweet baby Jesus, he is like a model I would see in magazines. His eyes slightly widen as he stares at me and he steps forward in my direction before a guy slightly behind him with dark brown hair and eyes grab his arm stopping him.

They all make their way up to seats in the bleachers and multiple guys from the group meet my eyes for a split second. Multiple other girls stare at them as they make their way up and I know Rose was too as she says, "Now that is a man. Is there somewhere I can to buy one?"

I turn my attention to Rose, scoffing. "He's probably an ass," and I give her a pointed look. "As you would know."

I ignore the feeling of being stared at, knowing my mind is playing tricks on me. I swallow and I catch my breath.

A lady moves to the middle of the gym, her smile big, with a mic in her hands. "Alright, ladies and gentlemen, today is the annual archery competition. These archers behind me have all worked hard to hopefully move forward today to Cities. This is a five-minute warning for the archers to get ready before we begin."

The lady walks off to the judging table and I grab my quiver, slinging it across my back. I put on my black arm guard and then a black handguard that covers only my index finger and thumb. I grab my bow and I stand there waiting to be called.

Five minutes later, the competition has started and I watch the archers who go before me. Most have either gotten close to bulls-eye or have and I feel a knot form in my stomach.

"Elizabeth Kennedy."

At the sound of my name being called, I take a deep breath. Rose gives me a fist bump before I walk up to my first target.

I load my arrow drawing it slowly back. I slow my breathing despite my nerves. I stare at my target and at the intake of a breath, I let the arrow fly hitting the bulls-eye. I feel a smile form on my face when I move to the second target that is farther. I do the same, hitting the target in the bulls-eye and I begin to feel my nerves melt away.

I stare at the third target, which is the farthest and as I load my arrow, taking aim, I see something shift in my peripheral vision. I take my focus off of the target to see the group of guys and the handsome boy all staring at me intently. I find myself staring at him and a small smirk forms on his lips.

I shake my head, refocusing on the target. I can feel their stares on me and my hands begin to slightly shake.

I lick my lips nervously and I take a breath, letting the arrow fly.

My breath catches, I just missed the bulls-eye. I stare at the target, surprised. I rarely miss, ever.

I turn my attention back to the group of men and I send them glares. This is their fault, they got me distracted.

I turn around making my way back to Rose who smiles at me. "Liz, you did an amazing job."

"Not as good as I want," I mumble.

"I saw those guys shifting in their seats and I would have

gotten distracted too. You still got very close."

"I can't do anything about it now. We'll just have to wait and see what score I got."

I look back to the group of guys as they make their way to exit the gym. Of course, now they leave. But before the boy leaves he turns around, smirks at me and then leaves.

"Did you see that?" I turn to Rosalyn who shrugs.

"The boy, he just smirked at me! Was he trying to make me mess up?"

"That god smirked at you?" Rosalyn smiles and laughs.

"This is not funny!" I say trying to hold in a laugh.

"Alright, alright. How about we go and get some drinks from the vending machine?"

With my turn done and the judges scoring, we head out into the hallway heading towards the vending machine.

As Rose gets us both iced tea, I hear hushed voices talking urgently around the corner. I peak past the corner to see the group of guys hurdled, talking in hushed voices.

"That's her. That's the Luna." The handsome black-haired boy says.

The brown-haired boy who held him back earlier speaks up, "Jason, Elizabeth is human."

I take a sharp intake of a breath and the boys look in my direction. I quickly move away. How in God's name did they hear that? They have to have incredible hearing.

Just as Rose grabs both of our drinks I grab Rose by the wrist.

"So, uh, where's the washroom? I need to tell you something. Now."

"Well, where's the GPS?"

2. RUN

"He said what?"

I'm currently stuck in the girl's washroom with Rose as I tell her what I heard the guys said.

"Jason and his group of models. They said something about a Luna and they mentioned how I'm human."

Rose looks at me and then lifts her drink to her mouth. "This is the weirdest place ever. First the washrooms and now this."

"Washrooms?"

"Well, we did almost need a GPS."

"Oh, shut up! Let's just leave, I don't like how they're looking at me."

Rose's places down her drink and runs a hand through her auburn hair. "Is it the weird kind of freaky staring or the, I'm interested stare?"

"Really, Rose?"

She puts her hands up in defence. "Alright, alright. But what about the competition?"

I take a sharp intake of breath. "They can contact me if I leave early. I'm not happy with how I did anyway. There will be plenty of other competitions."

We begin walking out when Rose speaks up. "Also, I may have spent our cab money on food."

"You spent our way of getting back to the hotel on food?"

"Yes, food, something edible that your body needs to survive."

"I can't believe you."

We make our way back to the gym and we both begin packing up my stuff. I end up telling the judges that I wasn't feeling well and that I had to leave.

Rose and I speed walk our way out of the school. When we reach outside, the sun is beginning to set.

Since this school is surrounded by forest, we have some walking to do.

"You just had to get something to eat, didn't you?"

Rose and I currently walk on the side of a road with the forest to our left. The sun has almost set leaving us in the dark.

"Yes, yes I did."

About ten minutes later, the sun has finally set leaving us in the dark. A chilly breeze sends a shiver down my back.

I hear the noise of a car driving in our direction and we turn around to see a black Corvette and truck stop beside us. The window rolls down and I'm met with Jason and his manpack.

You have got to be kidding me.

"You need a ride?"

Rose opens her mouth but I grab her by her arm. "No, we're fine, thanks."

"It's quite dark out, not too safe for you two."

I laugh. "We can handle ourselves just fine, thank you."

A smile forms on his face but suddenly drops when we hear rustling in the woods behind us.

I search the forest and I readjust my quiver on my back. I hear more rustling before Rose steps back.

"Uh, I'll take your offer. Drive me home please."

I see a dark shadow move quickly in my vision and I grab my bow from Rose.

I hear the doors of both cars opening and closing and soon the guys are standing in front of me with their backs to me, facing the forest. Jason is by my side and reaches out for my arm but thinks otherwise.

"Get in the car."

"And that is exactly how one would get abducted." Rose has already happily taken a seat in the car while I stand there ready to see what is making the rustling.

I hear a low inhuman growl come from the boys in front of me and past them, I see pairs of glowing red eyes.

I squint into the forest, trying to make out the creature or thing. "What the hell . . ."

"Elizabeth, get in the car!"

The red eyes are suddenly closer and Jason moves forward.

"Alec, get her in the car!"

I'm suddenly dragged into the car by the boy with brown hair and he slams the car door shut. The car doors lock, and the only noise is our heavy breathing. All the boys ran into the forest, leaving Rose and I stuck in a car.

"What the hell was that?"

Rose shakes her head. "I don't know."

"All I saw were glowing red eyes. And the boys, they . . . growled. Something inhuman."

"What a joke."

"I'm not staying in some random guys car as they chase a loose animal." I unlock the car, opening the door as Rose follows from behind.

It's quiet as if all that just happened was part of my imagination.

"Well, that was entertaining. At least we know their prankers," Rose speaks up.

I shake my head, following along the edge of the road to get out of this neighbourhood.

Rose hums some melodic tune to break the silence, not that I mind. It's when she suddenly stops humming.

I hear a low inhuman growl come behind me and I swallow heavily seeing Rose's eyes widen. She takes a sharp intake of breath and goes deadly still before whispering, "Liz, don't move."

I hear the growling get louder and closer and when Rose's eyes widen even more, I turn around to see a huge brown wolf with glowing red eyes.

It suddenly lunges forward and both of us drop to the ground. I grab Rose by the hand.

"Run!"

We sprint into the woods, but I can hear the crunch of leaves and panting not far behind. I remember the spare hunting knife I have in my quiver and I reach back for it, gripping it tightly.

I stop, turning around, facing the wolf running straight for me.

"Come on!" I yell feeling a rush of adrenaline pump through

me.

Just as it lunges for me, I pierce the knife forward and the body of the wolf lands right on top of me. It snaps at my face, canines and all and I bury the knife deeper feeling hot, red blood run down hand hands and onto my face.

The red glow in the wolfs eyes fade and it goes limp on top of me.

I let out a gasp, breathing heavy as I try moving out from under the wolf, but its weight crushes me from underneath. I feel tears form in my eyes and my hands shake, trying to calm the panic blooming in my chest.

I let out a grunt as I grip the soil from underneath me to try and move but I can't. The wolf's body is too heavy.

I hear footsteps nearby and my body freezes. Please let it be Rose, I pray.

My heart feels like it's going to jump out of my chest and my breaths come out short with the weight on me. But as the footsteps get closer, I realize there are multiple people and I soon see Jason and the rest of his friends come into view.

"Elizabeth?"

I grit my teeth. "Please, help."

Jason signs for the guys to help and when the wolfs body is lifted off, I gasp for air. Jason kneels beside at his eyes check for any injuries.

"W-what was that?"

Jason looks behind him at the rest of the guys and they seem to be having their own conversation through their facial expressions.

"We found Rose. She's back in the car."

I look between them all, deciding if they're a threat. I nod silently as he helps me up. "Now let's get you out of here."

Jason and Alec are in the front of the car while Rose and I sit in the back silently. Behind us is a truck driving behind us with the rest of the boys.

The whole car ride is silent and despite everything that's happened, I find my eyelids growing heavy.

I can see Jason look at me in the rear-view mirror and his features soften despite his hard grip on the steering wheel.

I focus my attention to the window, watching to make sure we'll be okay. But at some point, my eyelids get too heavy and I fall asleep.

3. A NEW WORLD

I hear the car door open on my side, but I don't move feeling too exhausted. I feel an arm behind my knees and another arm wrap around my back.

I feel myself get picked up and I open my eyes slightly to see Jason looking down at me.

"It's okay."

I nod slightly, closing my eyes and I subconsciously move closer to him. I slowly fall back asleep to the rock of his footsteps.

I wake with the glare from the sun and I shield my eyes.

"Rose, why did you open the blinds?"

When I get no response, I open my eyes realizing I'm not in the hotel room.

I'm currently in a large bed with grey bed sheets. Dark brown paint covers the wall with brown hardwood floors. Floor to wall windows covers the wall to my right overlooking a forest and grey skies.

I almost stumble out of bed while looking at the view, it's beautiful.

I look down at myself and I'm still wearing the same clothes: black leggings and a red shirt. I walk around barefoot towards a door and inside is the biggest walk-in closet I've ever seen in my life. One side is filled with clothes but the other side is completely empty.

I head to another door and it's a huge bathroom. White tile and cabinetry a with grey countertops. Everything is so sleek, clean, fresh.

I retreat back into the room heading to the final door. I find my black boots at the edge of the bed and I quickly put those on.

I leave the room into an empty, quiet hallway.

Hmm, left or right?

I randomly take a right hoping that maybe I'll be able to get out of here and find Rose.

Then I remember who took me here in the first place: Jason and his model boy club. And he carried me last night.

I need to get out of here.

After endless turns, I slouch against the wall. This place is like a freaking castle and where the hell is everyone?

I let out a frustrated yell before standing back up. It's like a maze in here.

I finally hear multiple voices and the sound of feet pounding against the wooden floor. It sounds like they're in a rush.

As I hear them getting closer, I open the door across from me and I leave a crack open so I can still see.

Multiple guys rush by as if they're searching for something. One stops in front of my door and . . . sniffs the air.

What the hell?

Suddenly, a hand clamps down over my mouth and just as I'm about to headbutt that person, I get turned around to see Roses frantic eyes.

She hesitantly lets go of my mouth.

"Rose, thank God."

"We need to get out of here. We don't even know these guys."

Then it hits me, they didn't even take us to the hospital after what happened or the police station. They took us to their house. A house full of guys. Hot ones, but still.

"We need to leave, now."

Past her is a window and I move forward realizing it can be unlocked.

"I know what you're thinking, Liz. I am not doing it."

I completely ignore her. "We're what, two stories up? If we land properly, we should be okay, right?"

"I am not jumping out of a window!" Rose whispers harshly.

"We don't have a choice! Now come on!"

I open the window and I straddle the ledge. Below is a garden and a couple of bushes but that's it.

"Liz, you're crazy." Not a question, a statement.

"You are too. I'll see you at the bottom."

I don't think, knowing she will follow me , I just jump and with the bushes at the bottom and against the house, I feel the pain and sting of sticks and thorns piercing my skin and causing scraps and bruising. I fall, my legs giving out underneath me from the impact. I hear Rose fall down behind me, but I'm too focused on what's in front of me.

The place we were just in is surrounded by a tall black gate and multiple people in black uniforms stand along it on guard. But that's as normal as it gets. Multiple huge wolves walk along on the outside of the gate and both Rose and I stand in shock.

"Is that . . ." Rose starts but I finish.

"A wolf?" I finish.

Suddenly, all the people in black uniforms are on guard, eyes searching for something or someone. A guard spots us and his eyes widen.

"Luna!"

I turn to Rose. "Did he just call me Luna?"

Rose grabs me by the wrist as multiple guards soon come running after us.

We run across the grass running down a hill when suddenly a black and brown wolf cut in front of us. I trip over my own two feet feeling my ankle twist and I fall, rolling down the hill.

I scream, covering my face with my arms.

By the time I've stopped rolling, my chest is heaving up and down for me to catch my breath. I lay there, staring up at the sky. The cuts on my arms and legs sting and my ankle throbs in pain. And to top it off, I'm covered in dirt and still dried up blood from the wolf from yesterday.

I prop up on my elbows to see both wolves in front of me. My breath catches and I find myself frozen in spot. The black one is almost as tall as me standing and its eyes . . . wait a minute, I know those eyes.

"Jason?"

The wolf sits down as if in acknowledgement and the brown wolf beside him bows its head at me. The brown fur and eyes are the same ones as Alec.

"Alec?"

The wolf looks up and I find the world suddenly spinning. "Oh my God. You two—you're wolves. Werewolves."

The black wolf moves forward but I put my hand up. "Don't, I—I need a minute."

Wolves. These guys are all freaking wolves, and seeing it right in front of me was enough for me to black out.

I wake in the same bed only though this time I'm not alone in the room. Alec sits beside the bed, eyes on me while two more people guard the door.

I sit higher up remembering everything that happened.

"Jason's on his way."

I move across the bed, getting as far away from them as I can. Alec sits in a chair, arms crossed over his chest.

"So, you're all—"

"Werewolves, yes."

A small part of me wished it was a dream but of course not.

Suddenly, the door opens, and Jason walks in. He wears all black but it suits him very nicely and I find my eyes roaming body. This boy is something.

"You're awake." Jason pulls another chair beside Alec before releasing a breath. "How are you feeling?"

I hold my head. "This is not real! This is a sick joke and I want you to take me home or I'm calling the police! Why am I here? And where's Rose?"

"Rose is fine, just sleeping everything off. And if I were to tell you why you were truly here, I think you would freak out even more."

I laugh. "I just found out that supposedly werewolves exist. Mine as well keep the pranks coming."

Jason shares a look with Alec before turning to me. "This is *not* a prank. Let's just say that there's a whole new world that you don't even know about. Everything about werewolves, vampires, witches, enchanters, they're all true. Right now, you're at my pack, Night Shade in the werewolf colony. I am the Alpha, in this case, the leader of this pack. Throughout the werewolf, colony are multiple other packs run by other Alphas but here, Night Shade is basically the Capital, the strongest. In other words, I'm the King of all the Alphas in the werewolf colony. Surrounding us are other colonies, Vampire, Witch, Faerie and Enchanters."

Jason stops, letting me take this all in. "Are you following?"

I hang my mouth open. "You really put a lot of research into this didn't you?"

Jason ignores my comment. "Every werewolf has a mate. Every wolf is always on the look for their mate, their other half, their true love. Mates are chosen by the Moon Goddess so unlike in your world, here our true loves are chosen. Almost like fate. And you Elizabeth, are my mate, the Luna of the Night Shade pack.

4. FATE VS. REALITY

I laugh. After everything Jason just told me, I laugh.

"This has got to be some kind of joke. I mean, I can't be your *mate*, I'm human."

"The Moon Goddess doesn't make mistakes. It's fate."

"Okay, you all seriously have mental issues, so I'm going to grab my friend and return to my work, reality."

"Well," Jason moves closer to me and my breathing intensifies. He's even hotter up close.

Oh dear Lord.

I can feel heat rushing to my cheeks, the palms of my hands getting sweaty.

Jason leans in whispering into my ear. "You're in my world and here, fate does exist." He pulls back, a smirk tugs on his lips. "You're cute when you blush."

I turn away from. He looks at Alec and both of their eyes go distant, not focused for a second, then it goes away and they look at me.

"Elizabeth, Alec here is my beta, second in command here. I trust him with everything and he's also here to protect you when I cannot."

I laugh, "Yeah, okay."

Alec bows his head slightly. "It's wonderful that we finally found you."

I turn to Jason, growing serious. "You can stop with the act."

Jason stays silent.

"You can't be serious."

They continue to stay silent.

"So, I really am your mate then?"

Jason nods. "Since you're human, there's so much for you to know and learn," he leans in, his voice quieter and deeper. "And that makes everything so much more interesting."

"You all are crazy."

Suddenly, Jason looks back at Alec, a cold expression taking over.

"Dammit," Jason mutters under his breath.

Alec suddenly leaves the room yelling out orders when Jason turns to me. "We have rogues entering our borders, we don't want them getting any closer so I told Alec and some of the guards to deal with it."

"Rogues? And how did you tell them? You were with me the whole time."

Jason smiles. "Just like I said, this is going to be interesting telling you everything."

When evening came, Rose came and visited me with some bad news.

"We should have been home by now. My parents already called wondering why we're not back."

And just like that, we're back into reality.

"What did you say?"

"I said that you're sick so we're staying a bit longer before travelling back. That's like maybe three or four days max before they come down themselves."

I drag a hand down my face. "What are we going to tell them? Yeah, hey mom, I found out that I'm the King of Alphas mate so I'll be staying here. Sorry."

Rose almost laughs.

"See! She'll think I've lost it too."

I throw my hands helplessly into the air.

"How's your ankle?"

I've been stuck lying down in bed for most of the day because I ended up spraining it when I fell down.

"Not too bad. Just sore."

"So what's the game plan?"

I shrug. I really don't know what's going to happen. I just found out I'm a Luna to the biggest pack—supposedly.

Rose gives me a look. "You're not actually going to stay, are you? We have a life back at home to get to."

I look around the room. "I can't just leave this, Rose."

"You mean you won't leave Jason?"

"What? No!"

"You don't want to leave because you like how hot he is," Rose mumbles.

"No! I found out I'm the Luna for this pack, Rose. The mate to Jason who is like a king here. That's a big deal."

"So what, are you just going to throw your old life away now for some psycho who believes you're his mate? Liz, they are crazy."

I scrunch my eyebrows together.

"Well, I can't stay here. Your mom doesn't live here. What about everyone else at home, what about archery and all those competitions? Are you just going to forget about it because of your basically bound to a man by some werewolf fate?"

I open my mouth to speak but nothing comes out.

"Look, this is reality. You can't just throw everything you worked for away. We need to call the cops.

Rose then moves to the back of the room picking up my bow Jason brought back to me. She places it down on the bed.

"Don't leave your world behind for *fate*. You make your life, you choose what you want, not some Moon Goddess mumbo jumbo."

I look down at the bow and I pick it up feeling the smooth curve as I run my fingers along it. As I do this, I hear the door shut close realizing that Rose left me here alone.

Around seven, a lady comes into my room with a tray of food for dinner. Even though I'm starving, I want to know why Jason has just left me here or why Alec hasn't come.

"Um, excuse me?"

The lady turns around before shutting the door and smiles. "Yes, Luna?"

I forget that they call me Luna in this place. "Do you know where Jason is?"

Her smile grows bigger. "Alpha Jason is dealing with the rogues that crossed the border with Beta Alec. Would you like me to send a message to him?"

"No, it's fine, thank you."

Once the lady leaves and I've finished dinner, I attempt to walk.

My ankle is still swollen but I can't just sit around here all day. I need to talk to Rose.

I slowly apply pressure to my ankle but hiss in pain.

Alright, I guess I'm crawling.

I'm on my hands and knees, following the directions Rose gave me if I needed to find her.

When I arrive at her door and I knock on it, no reply comes.

"Rose? It's Liz, can we talk?"

But still, no reply.

I open the door slowly. "Rose."

When I enter the room, she's not there. But on the bed is a piece of paper.

Liz,

I've gone to get help. Stay here and play around until the police arrive. I'll let your mom know you're okay.

Let that arrow fly.

Your best friend,
Rose

I take a seat on the bed, holding the letter. I don't know how long I stared at it, but I couldn't believe it.

Rose left.

5. INTERROGATION

JASON

"Why did you come here?"

I currently stand outside the cells that house all the criminals and rogues. Alec and the guards caught the rogues that crossed into my pack and now I'm stuck interrogating when I can be with Elizabeth.

"Hurry up." My wolf Ace says.

"I asked you a question."

Both male rogues sit there and I see their shoulders slightly shake. Are they laughing?

I clench my fists and I signal to Alec to open the cell. I move swiftly, grabbing both men by the collars of their shirts. I let out a growl and they bow their heads down.

"Do not make me ask again."

The one rogue looks up at me with an amused expression. "I can smell human on you, Jason."

"You address me as, Alpha." I can feel my anger rise.

"Do you really think you could hide bringing a human here? I can smell her on you. No one ever brings humans here unless for a very important reason. I wonder what."

The other rogue laughs and I slam him against the wall.

The other rogue's eyes widen before a smirk forms. "We all know that human is your mate. And it's been so long since we saw an actual human."

I drop the man on the ground before running out of the cells.

Alec runs by my side as I mind link my guards at home. "Find Elizabeth and stay there until I arrive."

6. MISSING

Elizabeth

I sit on the bed, still staring at Rose's note.

She left.

Suddenly, the door bursts open and Jason and Alec walk in with five guards behind them. Jason walks up to me before embracing me.

My arms stay at my side, staying as still as a statue.

"Thank God." I hear him mutter.

I can see Alec and the guards looking around the room when Jason pulls away.

"What's going on?" I sceptically ask.

"The rogues, they know you're here, they can smell your scent."

Jason turns around running a hand through his hair.

"Rogues?"

Alec speaks up, "Basically wolves who belong in no pack and are on the run."

I can see Jason's hands clench, almost turning white. "They know you're human. They see that as an opportunity to get to me now and they think they can easily get their hands on you."

"I'll watch her, Alpha. I think either you or me should watch her with at least five guards until the news of you finding your mate dies down." Alec then looks over at me and gives a small smile. "I also wouldn't mind getting to know the Luna a bit more."

Jason nods. "I think that's a good idea." He then looks down and see's the note in my hand. "What's that?"

I crumple the letter in my hand. "Just doodling."

Jason walks over and kneels in front of me while Alec and the guards move out of the room. "How's the ankle?" Jason grabs it with gentle hands.

"It's still swollen," I say pulling it out of his hands.

"I'm not used to this. You humans heal so much slower."

I laugh. "Yeah, we have to endure pain."

Jason looks up at me and he gently places my ankle down. I feel heat rise to my cheeks when his hand moves up from my ankle to my leg. Even though it's a simple touch I find myself closing my eyes, enjoying the tingles spreading through my body.

"You should sleep," Jason says standing up.

I re-open my eyes and I nod.

"My younger sister has some clothes here for when she visits. I'll have someone drop some off for you."

"Thanks."

Two guards are outside your door. My room is just down to the left if you need me. Goodnight, Liz."

And just like that, he leaves and I'm alone once again.

A buzzing noise interrupts my sleep as I wake up in the middle of the night. The shine from the moon spills into my room, the only light source.

I turn to my side to see Rose's cell phone buzzing. Rose's mom is calling me.

I grab it immediately. "Mrs Summers?"

"Rose?'

"No, it's Liz."

"Oh thank God I got hold of you. I'm sorry for calling at this hour but is Rose with you?"

I feel my stomach drop. "She left today to go back home. She should be home by now."

"She never came home, Elizabeth. The last text I got from her was that she was on her way home and that she needed help. I tried calling her but she won't pick up."

My mouth runs dry. Thoughts run through my head. What if Rose never really did leave, or someone took her? What if she did try leaving and a wolf saw her or she crossed a boundary line into another colony by accident. And she's all alone.

"Oh, God."

I tell Mrs Summers to call the police and I stumble out of bed. I open the door and both guards outside my door immediately turn to me. I wince when I put pressure on my ankle but I ignore it.

"Luna, is something wrong?"

"Get me, Jason."

Not even a second later, I hear footsteps coming from my left to see Jason walking towards me shirtless.

I breath in deeply, eyes up, Liz, eye up."

"What's wrong, Sweetheart?"

I clench my jaw. "First of all do not call me that. I am *not* your sweetheart. Second, Rose is missing. She never made it home."

"How do you know?"

I hold up Rose's cell phone. "Her mom called. Jason, I'm scared, what if something happened, or a wolf got her or—"

Jason moves toward his desk. "I would know if she was still in my territory. And my wolves wouldn't attack her. No rogue could have gotten her because I was with them in the cells."

My blood suddenly runs cold.. "Jason, you said the rogues smelled humans right? You came back in a rush because you thought something happened to me. Was anyone with Rose?"

I look up at Jason frantically but he stays quiet. "You left her all alone?"

"I—" Jason starts but nothing comes out.

"Rose didn't leave, I know she would never do that. Those rogues were a distraction. They came for me, but they got the wrong girl. We're both human and she could have had my scent on her because I'm always around her."

I take a step back feeling tears form in my eyes. "They think Rose is the Luna."

A minute later, Alec round the corner holding a red piece of fabric and he hands it to Jason before turning to me with sad eyes.

I can see a marking on the red piece of fabric. White fangs.

"The guards and I found this in her room. We know who took her."

I suddenly make the connection for what's on the piece of

fabric and I already know what Alec is going to say.

"Vampires."

He almost spits out the word before turning to Jason. "Those bloodsuckers haven't stopped trying to take over this colony."

"Vampires!" I exclaim.

Jason turns to Alec. "I want to know how the hell they got in here in the first place."

"Vampires are real?"

Alec shakes his head, ignoring me. "They could've had help from someone on the inside. I'm not sure but I will check everyone."

"Real, all of it," I state in shock. Time seems to be slow.

"I want you to double out border patrol and find out any idea of who could have helped. Either Liz will be with me or you at all times. I'm not leaving her alone without a guard."

Alec and his guards nod as Jason gives out his orders. "And contact the leader of the Vampire Clan. Let him know, Alpha Jason needs to speak with him immediately. He messed with the wrong pack.

7. COLD BLOODED

It was cold. Breathtakingly cold as I stood there in the forest with snow falling from the sky. I'm barefoot and the snow almost now burns my feet. My arms are so cold that the snow feels like it burns when it lands on me. So pretty, but it can be so deadly.

I rub my arms trying to create some warmth as I stand in my shirt and shorts when suddenly I hear some rustling nearby. I turn around in the direction of the noise feeling my heart beat faster.

"Hello?"

Suddenly the same brown wolf with red eyes I killed is walking towards me, snarling and growling.

I back away slowly with my arms out.

"I'm sorry."

It comes closer.

"No, stay back."

Closer.

Suddenly, the same knife in my hands. I thrust it forward in front of me.

"I said stay back!"

The wolf lunges for me and I scream.

"Elizabeth!"

Suddenly, I'm bolting up in bed into a pair of arms. My palms and forehead are sweaty and I realize that I'm shaking and someone is embracing me.

"Jason?" My voice sounds raw as if I was actually screaming.

He pulls away giving me a small smile. "I'm here. You nearly gave me a heart attack when I heard you scream." He tucks a strand of hair behind my ear and his fingertips just brush against my neck.

So I really did scream then.

Jason stares at me intently. "Do you usually get nightmares?"

I shake my head.

"Do you want to talk about it."

I open my mouth but I close it again. "No, it's okay."

"You should still try going back to bed, Liz."

I nod my head but when he moves away I grab onto him again and he looks as surprised as me. "Can you stay here? At least until I fall asleep?"

He nods, not saying a word and grabs a seat, sitting at my bedside, respecting my boundaries. I close my eyes feeling safe knowing that he is here and I fall asleep.

I wake up alone with a note on the nightstand beside me.

Liz,

Went out to have the call with the Vampire Clan leader. Alec is outside your door to guard you while I am gone. Relax today, you deserve it.

Jason

I attentively make my way to my bathroom to draw myself a nice warm bath.

As I lie there, I begin to feel relaxed until thoughts of Rose and home enter my thoughts. I can't imagine what will happen to Rose if she actually got hurt. And I still don't know how I'm going to tell my mom about all of . . . this.

When I get out of the bath, I realize I have no new clothes to change into.

Dammit.

I wrap a towel around me and when I open the door, Alec is standing there and his eyes widen.

"Luna, uh, what can I do for you?"

"Jason said his younger sister has some spare clothes."

"I'll take you to her room so you can pick something out."

"Thank you."

It's difficult keeping up with Alec's long strides, especially with my ankle. He seems to notice though and begins to slow down.

After some moments of silence, I speak up. "So, is it usually this quiet in the house."

"Actually it's usually a lot louder. We'd usually have staff and guards running around. But Jason wants you to be comfortable after everything he told you about us so he thought you could use some quiet time and relaxing. He also doesn't want you to worry about Rose."

"That's really nice of him."

"He really cares for you and will do everything and anything for you. You are his mate. And since you are the Luna, everyone will basically do whatever you say."

I turn to him shocked. "Seriously? I have that kind of power?"

Alec nods with a smile. "You're pretty important here. And since you're human, you're more . . . fragile. So that's why you'll be seeing a lot of me around or the guards."

We arrive in Jason's sister's room and I quickly put on an outfit: black jeans, and a blue sweater.

The sweater is slightly smaller then what I would usually wear but it still fits nicely.

I put my hair up into a messy bun and then I'm done. I turn to Alec and I put my hands on my hips.

"Alright, so now onto our next adventure. Where's the kitchen?"

I possibly just had the best breakfast. When we arrived in the kitchen, Jason has his own personal chef so I was able to order whatever I wanted. In the end, I ended up having red velvet pancakes and chocolate milk. I'm probably going to get so fat.

"So, what would the Luna like to do today?"

"Alec, just call me Liz. No need for formalities."

Alec almost looks bewildered. "I am going to call you Luna because it is an honour for me to be guarding you and I want people to know that."

"Alright fine. But I can't really do anything. Not with my ankle."

"Oh yeah, you humans heal so slowly. I keep forgetting. Jason might be able to help you out. He has some healing powers but it drains him."

"What? That's awesome!"

"Not everyone has that talent. It's one of many he has."

"I do wish I could do some archery."

"We could set up some targets for you or—"

Alec suddenly stops talking and his eyes go distant for a second before returning.

"Jason is on his way. He spoke to the Vampires. They have Rose."

"Three vampires will be crossing to deliver Rose back to us. They don't want to mess with any of us or start a war over here and they found out she wasn't the actual Luna. They said she's perfectly fine but Vampires have a thing for lying."

Alec and I stand in the living room currently as Jason tells us what happened. Vampires are total idiots it seems.

"So when are they coming?"

Jason looks down at his wristwatch. "Vampires move fast but they don't really like doing business during the day. They should be here by tonight. I doubled my guards at the wall so they will let me know."

Rose is coming back, she's alright.

I nod, taking a seat on the couch. "Thank God she's okay."

Jason, Alec, me and about ten guards all wait outside the house for when the three vampires arrive with Rose.

They arrive in a swift move, within the blink of an eye and Rose stands among them with her head down but she seems different. She's as pale as the vampires around her.

"You said she was okay."

The one vampire smiles. "And she is. Rose, why don't you tell them."

Rose lifts up her head slowly and I realize the ring in her eyes that were once green are now glowing red as dark as blood, her skin is as pale as snow and when she smiles, two fangs show.

"No," I whisper feeling tears form in my eyes.

Rose smiles. "Hey, guys. I've been *dying* to see you again."

I move forward but Jason puts an arm out in front of me.

"What did they do to you? Rose, I'm so sorry."

"Oh no." Rose puts up her index finger moving it side to side. "Don't apologize, silly. In fact, I want to thank you. Because of you, I've never felt so alive. Actually wait no, I'm dead." She hits herself on the side of her head with the palm of her hand. "That doesn't make any sense!"

She walks forward but the guards take a step forward and she whistles lowly. "I can't even hug my best friend? What a shame, I really did want to thank her. But Liz, I'm now super-fast, I can hypnotize people, I can make people do what I want and I can now eat whenever I want."

She looks down at me, but not as my friend, but almost as if I'm a price of meat.

"No," I repeat.

I stare at my friend feeling tears fall down my cheeks. The Rose I know is gone. Only a monster remains.

"Oh yes. Come here, I can show you what I mean. We can be friends forever."

She suddenly runs toward me but the guards all run at her protecting me. Everything seems to happen within the blink of an eye as. Jason pushes me behind him and I see Alec shift into his wolf at my side.

In seconds the three vampires are on the ground, officially dead if that makes any sense. Two guards hold Rose down on the ground and she stares at me with wide red eyes.

"You smell so good, Liz. Can I please take one bite?"

I turn away, closing my eyes.

Take her to the cells while we figure something out," Jason orders.

Rose gets dragged away, screaming and laughing historically. I stand there, turning to Jason.

"They killed her."

Jason moves to wraps his arms around me but I push him

away.

"Your stupid world and your stupid colony!" I shove him. "You did this to her!" Tears fall freely down my face and Jason holds me tighter, letting me cry. They destroyed the Rose I knew.

"Because of you . . . " She said.

And it is true. All of this is my fault

8. LEARNING

I sit at the kitchen table as Jason and Alec talk silently in the living room about what to do with Rose.

She's a vampire and she wanted to actually eat me. That was not my friend.

I put my head in my hands and I close my eyes taking a deep breath.

What am I going to tell her mom? What am I going to tell my mom?

I feel more tears form in my eyes. I can't believe this happened.

I suddenly feel a warm hand on my shoulder and I look up to see Jason handing me a cup of coffee.

"Thanks."

Jason pulls a seat out beside me. "Alec has left for the night to get some rest. Right now we're going to keep Rose in one of the cells until we can figure something out."

I clench my mug and my knuckles go white. "What is there to figure out, Jason. She's dead. She has no beating heart. We saw her, she's gone crazy. She wanted to sink her teeth into my neck!"

Jason puts a hand on my hand that's holding the mug. He pries my fingers off of it and holds my hand in his. I look up at him with tears eyes. "What can we do, Jason? What options are there?"

"The Vampires are a complicated colony. They multiply quickly but when they get a newborn, they don't seem to realize that they're dead, they actually think they're still alive. Rose acted the way she did because she's not used to what's happening to her. Her human body is adjusting to vampires and her mind is taking everything in. Give it a couple days and she'll start to settle down. The Rose you know should start to slowly come back but she won't be entirely the same."

I nod my head. "It could have been me."

"And thank God it wasn't. If it were you I'd be over in the

Vampire colony with my whole pack."

"What do I tell her mom?"

Jason's eyes soften and he squeezes my hand. "Rose will have a hard time controlling her thirst for blood. But even so, going back to the humans is like handing her a buffet. It can't happen."

I feel my chest tighten. "She can never go back home. The police won't stop searching for her until they think that she's dead. That's what's going to happen, isn't it?"

Jason nods and I close my eyes letting out a breath. "I'm so tired, all I wanted was for Rose to be okay."

"And she will be. But you still need to take care of yourself. It's midnight, let's get you to bed."

I'm about to protest but he picks me up. I rest my head against his chest and I close my eyes falling asleep.

When I wake up, I see Jason sleeping in a chair in the corner of my room.

His features aren't as intense as they would be when he's ordering people around. In fact, he looks more like a boy. I throw my covers back and as I swing my legs around to the floor, I notice that bruising has formed on my ankle.

"Oh my God."

This wakes Jason up and he's immediately kneeling down beside me. studying my ankle with gentle hands.

I hiss in pain when he moves it slightly. "Sorry."

I sit up against the headboard on the bed and he takes a seat on the edge of the bed with my ankle in his lap.

"Can you move it at all?"

I move it slightly and pain shoots up my leg. I shake my head.

Jason takes a breath before gently placing both of his hands on my ankle. "Now I didn't want to do this because it hurts, but you're in more pain now."

"Wait, what are you doing?"

Jason's eyes turn darker and pain shoots up my legs. I grip the sheets underneath me and I bite the inside of my cheek. Soon, a soothing feeling takes over and I lean back with a sigh.

I look down, noticing the bruising is gone.

"How—what did you do?"

"Can you move it for me?"

I move my ankle realizing it doesn't hurt anymore.

"Perfect, you're good as new."

I look up at Jason who breathes slightly heavier but still smiles at me.

"Thank you."

I suddenly realize how close we are and I can see the curve of his lips, how blue his eyes are. I imagine my fingertips gently following the line of his jaw.

We move closer to each other and I can feel my heart beat faster and faster. And almost as if he can hear it, he smirks.

"Do I make you nervous, Elizabeth?"

The way he says my name, my full name, the way it rolls off his tongue, sends a chill down my back.

We're only inches apart and I can hear my heartbeat in my ears.

Thump thump, thump thump, thump thump.

Jason reaches out and tucks a strand of hair behind my ear. He then runs his hand down my ear to my neck and when he looks back up at me, he moves forward, closing the space in between us.

His lips are warm, soft and gentle. When he pulls away looking into my eyes to see if that was okay, I grab the collar of his shirt and bring him close again.

Despite everything that's happened, I find myself forgetting everything. Almost like Jason is taking away my pain and hurt with this kiss.

When we pull away, my head is spinning and I find myself struggling to figure out how we even lead to this. I put my fingertips to my lips and a smile forms on my lips. I look up at Jason as he sits there.

"Wow." A smile forms on his lips and I feel heat rising to my cheeks. But then questions cross my mind.

"Jason, what is this whole mate thing? You never really explained it."

Jason scratches the back of his neck. "Well, when you find your mate, usually the male wolf will mark the female right away."

"Mark?"

"It's a way of showing other wolves that you're mine. I would bite your skin right," Jason runs a finger on the skin that connects my shoulder and neck, "here. It creates a bond between the male and female. We can hear each other's thoughts, feel each other's feelings and pain."

I stared at him wide-eyed. "You bite me? Wouldn't that hurt? This sounds really deep."

Jason laughs. "I would make sure it wouldn't hurt that bad."

"You said they do it right away. Have you ever been close to doing it to me?"

"When I saw you at the archery tournament, my wolf, Ace wanted to mark you right then and there. But Alec stopped me when I realized that you're human. So I've just controlled my wolf, waiting until you're ready."

I remember when I first saw Jason when he saw me he stepped forward in my direction but Alec stopped him.

"Is that all to it then?"

Jason stands up and looks around the room. "Well, there is one thing more that completes the mating process."

I stay quiet waiting for him to finish but he stands there. "To finish, uh, well, they both . . . "

I realize what he's going to say and I stand up abruptly, blushing. "No, absolutely not!"

Jason breaks out laughing and I turn around feeling heat rise to in my cheeks.

"I'm going for breakfast," I say leaving the room as quickly as possible.

Jason and I sit in the kitchen having our breakfast when he looks up at me. "You know, I don't really know much about you, Liz, besides that you love archery."

"There's not much to know. I mean, you know how much I love archery but besides that, I really don't do much. I'll usually read in my free time or go for a run."

"I can have Alec and the guys set up an archery range for you. But in the meantime, follow me."

Jason gets up and I follow him down multiple hallways before stopping in front of two large doors.

"I usually don't have time to come here but maybe it can be put to some use now that you're here."

He opens the doors and I almost forget how to breathe. A huge library is spread out before me. Bookshelves and windows covering floor to ceilings, sofas, chairs and desks filling the space.

"Jason, this is amazing."

I run my fingertips along the spines of books, waiting to get my hands on one.

"I have to go, Alec will be coming while I'm gone."

I grab a book and I take a seat in one of the chairs when he comes up and kisses me on the forehead.

"If you need anything, let Alec or the guards know."

I watch as Jason leaves before I open a book. My eyes scan the bookcases when I have an idea.

I look at all the book specifically looking for a couple. When I find them, I smile to myself before sitting down and opening up the first book called: Werewolf Creatures.

I'm met with many pictures of wolves as I dive in starting with knowledge on packs and leading ranks. Alpha is the leader with their mate called the Luna, then there are the Beta, Deltas and two Guardians who are supposedly a male and female who will guard the Alpha with their lives. From there they have healers, fighters and hunters who usually travel in groups of three. Then there's the rest of the pack and omegas who are close to getting kicked out.

I skim through more pages about their weaknesses and how they can't touch silver or have a plant called Wolfs Bane.

I then flip to a page about their lifestyles and enemies. It says werewolves have never gotten along with Vampires and will usually kill them on spot. A picture shows a wolf biting of a vampires head and a shiver runs down my spine.

It talks about how werewolves need their daily fitness and goes on pack runs. It says if they ever run into humans, they will attack and kill them or bite them to join their pack. Not all humans survive the transformation to become a wolf and end up losing their mind and dying. A picture shows a human down on all fours with glowing eyes. I swallow deeply when I turn the next page and my heart nearly stops.

It says that because the vampire colony is beside them, they try to keep peace with them by the werewolves taking humans into their cells and handing them over to the vampires to feed.

What if Rose was never taken? What if Jason and his pack handed her over? He said he had to leave but is he with Rose right now? If Vampires and Werewolves don't get along, is Rose in danger then?

"Luna?"

I slam the book shut and Alec steps into the library. "Uh, Alec, is everything okay?"

He looks at me wearily. "I was going to ask you the same thing. I could hear your heart beat beating faster."

"Oh, I'm fine." I try keeping my voice even and not shaky after what I just read. "Just getting into books that's all."

"Okay, well, I'll be out here if you need anything." He bows his head slightly and walks out.

I need to find Rose and get the hell out of here. Before she dies or I become a werewolf or fed to the Vampires.

9. CLAWS AND FANGS

Okay, calm down, Liz. My bow is upstairs in my room, if I leave tonight, I can get Rose and leave this place.

I can't stay here, even though all this information scares me, Rose was right, I have my own life I'm throwing behind.

I slowly exit the library where I'm met with Alec and two other guards.

"Luna." They all bow their heads in acknowledgement.

"I'm going to have some dinner and then head to bed, Alec. You can go home."

Alec smiles and crosses his arms as I walk away. "It's going to take a lot more than that to get rid of me. If I ever leave your side while Alpha Jason is out, he'll have my head."

I think back to the picture in the book, of the wolfs biting the heads of the vampires off.

A shiver runs down my back at the thought.

"Luna, are you alright?" He looks at me with concern in his eyes.

"You know what," I put a palm to my forehead. "I'm not really feeling the best. I'm just going to head to bed."

"Would you like me to get the pack Doctor?"

"No, it's fine. Just feeling a little under the weather," I lie.

I arrive outside my room to see Alec and the two guards. "You have permission to leave if you want to."

"Trust me, Luna," a guard speaks up. "It's an honour to guard you."

I give a small nod before entering my room.

Keep the heart rate normal or they'll think something is up.

The sun has almost set, and I know Jason will be home soon. I grab my bow and quiver, strapping it across my back.

I make my way to one of the windows that open and I straddle the edge of it as I look down. I pull my legs over and I jump.

I land quietly and as I make my way to the gate that

surrounds the house, guards nod at me and whenever they ask where I'm off to, I tell them archery practice. Many offered to accompany me, but I decline politely.

When the next guard comes my way, I ask them where Rose is. When they tell me she's in the cells and where that is, I smile to myself. They'll tell me anything because I'm Luna.

I walk down in the town for the first time and it almost looks like a regular human town besides from the occasional wolf walking around.

I walk down a path into the forest just as the guard had said and I arrive at an old, tall building.

Three guards stand outside the building and when I walk closer with my bow in hand and quiver on my back, they stand taller and now their heads.

"Luna? Alpha Jason didn't say you were visiting."

The man looks to be in his early twenties. He has blonde hair and blue eyes. He's tall and he's actually quite attractive.

I wave a hand and smile. "Oh, it's alright. Alec knows I'm here and he'll inform Jason for me."

I know that I won't have long. They'll probably mind-link each other and figure this all out.

"I'm Delta Sam, third in command here and I'm usually here at the cells. It's an honour to finally meet you, Luna."

I smile and nod. "I'm here to see my friend, Rose. She is here, right?"

Sam nods his head slowly. "Yes, I'm on orders by the Alpha to keep her secured with no visitors."

"Yes, well, she is my best friend and I would like to see her."

"If that is what you want. But I will accompany you."

Better than nothing. Sam turns around and leads me into the cells. It's dark and musty in the inside. Multiple guards line the walls, each bowing their head to their Luna.

We walk through a heavy metal door to where a large cell meets us. On the other side of the bars, is a small figure with her back to us.

I move forward but Same grabs me by the arm. "Be careful,

she's quite . . . energetic."

I nod before moving forward slowly. "Rose?"

When she doesn't respond I move forward more. "Rose, it's me, Liz, your best friend."

Her head slowly rises but she doesn't turn around. "Liz, I know you."

I move forward and I can almost touch the bars of the cell.

"Yes, you do. I'm your best friend."

"You smell good, Liz"

Rose then turns around, her red eyes focused on me. "Your scent is so . . . alluring, tempting."

She walks toward the cell bars with graceful movements.

"I've missed you."

A small smile forms on her lips. "I've missed you too, Liz"

And for a second, the Rose I know is there, but it quickly fades.

"Have they treated you well?" I ask.

She laughs. A cold, laugh. "I haven't been fed since I've gotten here. I need blood."

"Will you feel better if you do get blood?"

"Very much."

I turn to Sam but he shakes his head. "It's not allowed."

"I knew you were going to say that."

I roll up my arms sleeve, exposing my skin.

I turn to Rose and she stares at my arm, fangs already protruding from her mouth.

"Luna, no!"

Sam moves forward to grab me, but I thrust my arm in between the metal rods of the cell.

"I know Rose is still in there, I know she will stop."

At that moment, I feel a sharp piercing stab into my arm and I let out a gasp. I look over at Rose, seeing her teeth sink into my sink.

At first, it's pain but something takes over, it's almost soothing and I relax.

"Rose, let go of the Luna, now!"

I turn to Sam. "It's okay. She'll stop."

Sam runs a hand through his hair. "Goddess, she's going to make you attached. I've contacted Alpha Jason."

I feel myself become slightly dizzy and I turn to Rose who grips my arm.

A euphoric sensation takes over and I find myself giggling.

Sam tries grabbing me away but Rose has too much of a hold on me.

The dizziness intensifies and I look over at Rose.

"Rose, you need to stop now." My voice sounds far away.

I begin to feel hot, really hot and my movements seem sluggish, slow.

"Rose," I repeat.

She looks up at me and her eyes are pitch black.

"Rose, that's enough."

Sam growls from behind me, no doubt losing his mind seeing his Luna in this position.

Rose looks up at me again and her eyes return red and she lets go. Blood drips down her mouth.

My blood.

I look down my arm to see two puncture marks from where she bit me. Blood drips down my arm and I slump down to the ground.

The room spins around me.

"Liz, are you okay?"

I look up to see the Rose I know kneeling in front of me.

"The blood helped?" My words slur a little, but she nods. "My head is clear now, I can think. I was so hungry and all I could see rather than feel was just food. I'm sorry if I hurt you."

I shake my head. "I'm the one who should be sorry."

I turn to Sam who has kneeled beside me, helping me up.

"Let her out, please"

Sam looks at me like I'm crazy. "I don't think that's a good idea."

"Sam, let her out. That's an *order*."

Sam opens the cell door and Rose comes out embracing me.

My footing sways. "Are you okay, Luna?"

I turn to Sam and at that moment, the door opens and Jason, Alec and five other guards are behind them.

Without thinking, I draw an arrow, bringing my bow up with shaky hands.

My vision blurs and I can't seem to think straight.

"Liz," Jason holds up his hands and takes slow steps toward me. "What are you doing?"

My mind moves back to the book I read, about what they do to humans and I find myself drawing back the string even farther.

I see Alec moving slowly with his eyes trained on me. Everyone in the room focuses on me and the arrow.

What am I doing?

Focus, breathe.

They're evil.

"No!" I yell.

I feel sweat drip from my forehead and I see two sets of Jason instead of one. I shake my head and blink multiple times and when I look back up, Jason and everyone else in the room has glowing red eyes, like Rose.

My hands tremble, my heart beats faster and Jason notices. "Liz, deep breaths. We're not going to hurt you."

"I—I—don't"

Jason sniffs the air and his eyes move down to my arm dripping with blood. His eyes turn black and claws form in his hand when he looks up at Rose.

"You fed on her!? On a human!"

He takes a step forward but Rose hisses, crouching low, sensing Jason's threatening movements.

My arms begin to feel numb and I drop my bow. My legs turn to jelly and I see the ground coming closer.

I feel strong arms catch me before I hit the ground and I look up to see Jason.

You fed too much, Rose!" He moves his attention to me. "Don't worry, I got you. The pack Doctor is on his way."

I nod my head letting the darkness consume me

10. TRUTH

JASON

As Liz lost consciousness, I turn to Rose feeling anger boil underneath my skin and I can feel my wolf taking over.

She did this to our Mate.

"You did this." I use my Alpha tone and even though Rose is a Vampire, she bows her head backing off.

"I'm sorry, b—but she offered and I—I was losing my mind from n-not feeding."

It explains her behaviour. I've never seen or dealt with new Vampires. She must have acted the way she did because she was starving and losing her mind. Liz saved Rose.

I look down at my mate feeling my chest tighten. But why did she bring her bow with her?

Alec steps forward. "The doctor is at the packhouse."

I pick up Liz gently and Rose and Alec follow. Knowing that Rose is no longer her crazy self, I let her follow, but I will always have eyes on her.

As we walk out of the cells, I mind link Sam. "Get me, my Guardians. Have them meet me at the packhouse."

I look down at my mate and I kiss her forehead. When she wakes up, it's time to set some things straight.

I look over at Rose, watching her graceful, swift movements. She could run right now and attack my pack if she really wanted to, but Alec stays within reaching distance just in case her crazy ways come back.

"Can you control your thirst?"

Her fangs aren't showing anymore and her eyes aren't a glowing red anymore. It must be signs for when she does get hungry.

"I'm fine now. I should last a couple days before I need to feed."

I look over at Alec, mind-linking him. "We'll have to figure out a way to get her to feed. Maybe have some hunters go out with

41

her or retrieve something for her now and then."

Alec nods and by that time, we've reached the packhouse.

The doctor stands on the front steps with a female and a male healer.

"How long has she been out?" Doctor Andrews asks.

"Maybe ten minutes." I lay her down on the couch in the living room and I kneel by her side, holding her hand.

The doctor takes her pulse and the healers set up an ivy. "She's lost a lot of blood."

I turn to Rose, unable to keep my wolf at bay. "Look at what you did."

A healer walks in with two bags of blood and I immediately look at Alec and he moves to Rose, his body in front of her blocking the view. If Rose didn't turn that long ago, she's not going to be able to control herself. Even if she is satisfied and fed, the minute she sees blood, she could go out of control.

"Rose, breathe." I look over at Alec and I can see him gripping her shoulders.

"I can smell it. I—I need to leave."

Alec looks over at me and I can see Rose's eyes glowing red again. "Get her out of here, stay with her until she cools down and let me know when my guardians arrive."

Alec nods. "Yes, Alpha."

He takes Rose out of the room as they hook Liz up to blood. My heart breaks, I couldn't even protect my mate. I hold her hand and I kiss her knuckles.

I'm so sorry.

11. GUARDIAN

Elizabeth

I wake up feeling my hand being held by a warm hand.

I open my eyes slightly but then re-close them as I let out a groan feeling the worst headache in the world.

"Liz?"

I open my eyes again to see Jason by my side, holding my hand.

"You're awake." I'm suddenly crushed against Jason's chest and he nuzzles his face in the crook of my neck, breathing in my scent. I surprisingly wrap my arms around him missing his warmth, the feeling of safety. Then it all comes crashing down when I remember what happened. Me reading that book, attempting to get Rose and head back to the human colony and home. Then I passed out after Rose drank too much.

I let go of Jason and push him away slightly. He looks up at me confused and I cross my arms in front of my chest.

I look down at my hand noticing an iv. "First of all mister, you have some explaining to do."

"I do?"

"Second, I want to know that Rose is safe and in the packhouse."

"And thirdly, I need a glass of water."

After Jason went and got me a drink he told me he mind-linked Alec and told me he was with her and that she was sleeping at the moment.

"Is it true?" I ask.

He tilts his head to the side, confused as I continue. "When I was in the library, I read something on werewolves about how you take humans and give them to the Vampires so they can feed and you can keep the peace between your two lands. And if you didn't do that, you either kill us or turn us into one of you knowing that we may not survive the process."

Jason looks at me like I'm crazy as I'm telling him this. He raises an eyebrow. "And where did you read this?"

43

I shrug. "Some book in the library."

Jason's features soften and he takes a hold of my hand gently. "Liz, none of those are true. All those werewolf books are old, very, very old. None of those things happens today and if they did I wouldn't allow it. Most of those books are like history textbooks."

I feel myself relax a little. "So you didn't secretly take Rose to the Vampires then?"

Jason leans back, a smile forming on his face. "Oh, so that is why you went to the cells looking ready to kill an army. You thought we were responsible for her death and you went to get her and leave."

I wince at the word death, still not used to the fact the Rose is dead.

"I was scared."

Jason looks up at me and leans back towards me. He grabs my hand and kisses my knuckles. "There's no reason to be scared here. None of that is true. So please, if you want to learn more about us, just ask, don't read those dusty old stories."

I nod my head. "Okay."

His gaze flicks down to my lips and then back to my eyes. I still can't get over how blue his eyes are. I find myself leaning into him and when our lips touch, tingles spread and I pull away gasping, touching my lips. That didn't happen last time.

Jason laughs and gently kisses my forehead, more tingles spreading.

"What was that?"

"You're human, it takes longer for the mate bond to get stronger. You're starting to feel what it can do because you're liking me more and accepting the bond slowly. You can now feel this."

"Jason?"

"Yes?"

"I like you, but don't let it get to your head."

A smile spreads on his face and I feel heat rise to my cheeks. When did I become so bold and outspoken?

Alec walks into the room, stopping when he sees us looking at each other.

"Oh, um, Alpha, your guardians are here."

I remember that from the book. Maybe some things were true then. At least not the scary stuff. It said there were two, a male and a female who will protect the Alpha at all costs with their lives. They are the highest trained fighters and are so swift and quick that people barely put up a fight.

A tall male and female both walk in all black. The male has black hair and similar eyes to Jason. Actually, they look quite similar.

Jason turns to me with a smile on his face. "Liz, these are my guardians, they protect me with their lives. He gestures to the boy who is basically as tall and muscular as Jason. A scar runs down from his right eyebrow to the corner of his eye. I would think it's scary but he smiles at me and holds out his hand.

"I'm Thomas, Jason's younger brother."

Oh, so that's why they look so familiar. "I was wondering why you guys looked familiar." I laugh.

I then turn to the girl with a blonde braided braid. Her light blue eyes look down at me and she's pretty muscular for herself. She gives me a gentle smile despite her intimidating looks.

"I'm Ashley."

I shake hands with her and turn to Jason.

"My guardians have been out dealing with rogues lately. Now that we have more guards again, they're back and will usually be nearby, protecting us. Since you're here now, Ashley will be around with you at all times even if you're with Alec."

"Why so much protection?"

"We're having some problems with our neighbouring colonies. But don't worry, that's something for me to deal with. Right now, we need to set up a party letting the pack know that you're here."

I freeze in place. "What?"

"There's always a celebration for when a pack finds a Luna. Don't worry, you and Rose can go shopping if you like for what you want to wear."

I inwardly groan. I hate dressing up. If rather be in sweatpants or leggings with my hair up in a messy bun then in a dress with makeup and heels.

"Wonderful," I say trying to mask what I'm truly feeling.

An arm snakes around my waist and Jason pulls me closer. "Oh, we can all see how excited you are."

I roll my eyes.

"Oh and also," Jason rubs the back of his neck nervously. "My parents are coming by to visit and meet you. Today."

12. VISIT

"What?" I yell.

Jason puts his hands up and Thomas laughs.

"Nice one, Jason. Just telling her an hour before they come."

"An hour!"

Jason wears a sheepish look. "Well, I was going to tell you but then everything happened with you and Rose. They heard all the drama going on and decided to visit."

"Oh so now it's my fault?"

Thomas nudges Jason and Ashley laughs.

"No, it's not your fault—"

Ashley hooks her arm through mine. "Enough, you boys are ridiculous. Come on, Luna. Let's get you cleaned up and dressed. But then again we only have an hour because of a certain someone."

We turn around walking up the stairs and I can hear Thomas laugh and say, "Nice. Your mate is mad at you! Oh, this is going to be a great visit."

Ashley takes me to my room and tells me to sit at the foot of the bed while she gets something for me to wear.

"So besides from guarding me and putting your life on the line, you can also put my outfits together?"

Ashley laughs as she disappears into the closet. "Hey, I got a good eye for fashion. But let me just say, the clothes you are borrowing are totally not something I see you wearing. I'm surprised the Alpha hasn't taken you shopping."

I shrug my shoulders. "I guess your fashion skills will be put to the test."

Ashley laughs. "This is barely a test. I'm amazing when it comes to fashion, hair, and makeup."

"So you're a warrior but a girly girl underneath your badass appearance and weapons."

Ashley emerges from the closet holding clothes. "Precisely.

Now put this on. Times a ticking by."

I grab the clothes she gave me and change in the washroom. I change into black skinny jeans and a light blue blouse. The shoes are black ankle heals and I find the outfit works.

I walk out of the washroom to see Rose has joined Ashley and they both look at me, nodding me in approval.

"Rose!" I give her a hug and I forget that she's even a vampire. "You're not going to, you know, eat me, right?"

Rose laughs. "No, I'm quite in control now. Unless you get a nosebleed or something so let's hope you don't cut yourself or anything."

I laugh taking in Roses appearance. She's cleaned up, her light auburn hair in waves, her skin is paler then I'm used to. She has a nude-pinkish lipstick and her red eyes don't glow anymore.

"I'm glad you're here."

"Okay, okay, we need to finish getting you ready!" Ashley interrupts.

She grabs me by my shoulders and pushes me to sit down on the bed.

"Now, Jason's sister probably has some makeup and a curler we could use."

"Where is it?" Rose asks.

Down the hall, take a left, first door on the left.

Rose nods and disappears within the blink of an eye. She then returns not even a second later holding a bag of makeup and a curler in her hand.

I blink multiple times. "That was awesome."

Rose smile. "Some advantages to being dead I guess."

I feel my smile falter but nod.

Rose and Ashley apply some light makeup and curl the ends of my hair before I'm done.

I look at my appearance in the mirror. "You guys did a great job. Thank you."

Ashley looks down at her watch. "Alright, time to go. They should be here any minute."

Ashley walks ahead while Rose stays with me. I'm meeting Jason's parents, that's a pretty big deal to me.

"You're nervous." Rose stays and I look up at her.

"No, I'm not."

Rose narrows her eyes. "Yes, you are. I can smell the sweat on your hands. I can hear your heartbeat beating faster than normal. You're nervous."

A smile forms on her face and I roll my eyes. "So not fair, you using your vampire powers."

Ashley looks over her shoulder at us. "We all know your nervous, Luna."

"So not fair with you all using your wolf and vampire powers. Everyone can practically tell how I'm feeling."

Rose raises one eyebrow. "Any human could tell as well. Your un-clenching and clenching your hands, your licking your lips repeatedly and you fiddle with your hands. That is not a power, it's called being observant."

Before I can reply, we're standing in the living room seeing Jason, Alec and Thomas.

They all sit on the couch but when Jason looks up at me, his eyes turn darker.

I take a seat beside Jason and he leans over, his lips just touching my ear, "You look beautiful."

I feel heat rise to my cheeks. And I bite my bottom lip.

I hear a low growl come from Jason. "It's best if you don't do that, Liz."

I stop immediately. "So, uh, when are they going to arrive."

As if answering my question, a knock comes at the door and when Alec opens it, a lady with long brown hair walks in. Her features are soft. Jason has the same dark blue eyes as her. A man walks in after. He's tall with black hair, some strands of white and grey hair mixing in. His features are more sharp looking but when he looks at me and smiles, he doesn't seem as intimidating but more gentle.

"Mom, dad," Jason gently grabs my hand and leads me over to them. "Liz, these are my parents.

I hold out my hand to shake hers but she just takes me into a hug.

"Oh, you are so much more beautiful then what Jason said! I'm so happy he found you! I'm Brenda."

"Elizabeth," I say as she finally lets go of me.

I turn to the man and he smiles at me before giving me a more gentle hug.

"It's a pleasure to meet you. I'm Jonathan."

A minute later, a girl maybe in her early twenties walks in smiling. She has long brown hair in a ponytail with the same blue eyes. She gives me a hug, nearly lifting me off the ground. "So you must be my big old brother's mate. It's so great to meet you. I'm always stuck out training the Warriors that I have never gotten to meet you! I'm Rebecca, but you can just call me Becca."

I smile, "I'm Elizabeth, but most people just call me Liz."

Becca finally lets go of me before looking down at what I'm wearing. "Oh hey, that's my top! It looks a lot better on you than it ever did on me."

"I hope you don't mind, I haven't been able to get my own clothes yet."

She turns to look at Jason, her eyes wide. "You haven't taken your mate out shopping yet?!"

"It's been a little busy around here."

Her eyes then zero in on my neck. "Whoa, Jason you must seriously have some self-control if you haven't marked her yet."

Jason snakes a hand around my waist. "I'm not doing anything unless she gives me permission."

I smack his hand away.

"Alright," Rose says coming to my side. She claps her hands together. "Why don't we all sit down before they turn into a make-out session?"

Jonathan sniffs the air and his eyes narrow at Rose. "Vampire."

He moves forward with his claws extended and out of instinct, Rose's fangs extend and she hisses at him.

Without thinking, I step in between them. "Whoa, take it easy!

Rose is my friend."

"Vampires are our enemies."

Brenda puts a hand on her husband's chest and he calms down, his claws retracting. Rose backs off, her fangs retracting into her mouth. "Well Rose is not our enemy. She's my best friend and if you have a problem with that then we're going to have an issue here. Is there an issue?"

Jonathan's features soften. "I'm sorry, after being Alpha for so long and fighting an enemy for so long that stands right in front of you, you get defensive. But if the Luna say's you're not the enemy, then I believe it."

He extends a hand to Rose and she hesitantly takes it and shakes it.

As we all go to sit down, Jason leans down, whispering, "I like it when you take charge."

I smile but turn to everyone else to avoid the blush spreading across my cheeks. "Coffee anyone?"

A yawn escapes my mouth as we all sit in the living room exchanging stories. I've learned quite a lot about Jason. He's 21, his favourite colour is black, he likes going on pack runs and is quite adventurous.

Jason looks down at me, his arm around me with my head in the crook of his arm. "You tired?"

I nod, my eyelids feeling heavy.

Jason brings his attention to everyone in the room. Rose has already left, Thomas and Ashley stand along the wall of the room with their hands behind their back, and Brenda and Jonathan catch up with Becca.

"Hey guys, it's getting late so I'm going to take Liz upstairs."

"It was nice meeting you all. Goodnight."

They all wish me a good night as Jason and Ashley, my now assigned guardian following behind.

I sit down on the edge of the bed as Jason moves to the closet.

He comes back with some pj's and I walk to the washroom to change.

When I come out, he's sitting at the edge of the bed and gives a small smile. I sit beside him as he turns his gaze to me. He tucks a strand of hair behind my ear and looks down at my lips and then back to my eyes.

"Are you okay, Liz? I know that everything that's happened is a lot to take in."

I turn my gaze back to the floor. "I miss my mom, she must be worried sick by now. But at the same time, I feel safe with you now. Before I was terrified but now I find myself becoming more attached to you, I like your presence. You say it's fate, that we were chosen to be together. In my world, it doesn't happen that way. You got to kiss plenty of frogs before finding your prince. But here, I'm beginning to believe in fate because I'm beginning to feel strong feelings for you, and I'm terrified of that."

I turn my gaze back to Jason and he brings the palms of his hand to my cheeks and I bring my hands on top of his. "I'm so scared, Jason. Of all of this. I've just met you but I'm already feeling such strong feelings. But here, I've been made for you, I've been chosen to carry out the role of the Luna and knowing that means I can do it, that I can do this."

I bring my lips to his, feeling the warmth and softness of his lips. He moves in front of me and soon I'm lying down on my back, him on top of me never breaking the kiss. He moves his trail of kisses down my jaw and my neck.

Soon, Jason moves off of me, shaking his head. His eyes are now pitch black.

"What's wrong?"

"I have to stop. I can barely keep control of my wolf right now. If I don't I might end up marking you without your permission."

" What will it do?"

"We'd become connected. We'd be able to feel each other's emotions and feelings. If you ever got hurt or you needed me, I would know. If you were a wolf, we'd be able to communicate with our own mind-link, but because your human some things will be a little different."

"That's amazing," I find myself saying. "Where would it go?"

"Right," Jason drags his fingers lightly above the spot that was sensitive. "Here. But I won't do it unless you say it's okay. So that's why I have to stop or I'm going to lose control of my wolf and I'll accidentally mark you."

I nod my head. "Thank you."

He stands up pulling back the covers of my bed. "Now you need to get some sleep."

I crawl underneath the sheets and he tucks me in. "Ashley is outside your door guarding you. I'm just down the hall and Thomas will be outside my door. I'm not too far away."

I nod. "Goodnight, Jason."

"Goodnight, Liz."

13. THE COUNCIL

When I first woke, Jason told me about this council meeting that'll be happening today.

I have to go, I don't have a choice as a Luna but I'll be meeting the leader of every single colony. A pathetic human meeting supernatural creatures with amazing powers and abilities.

Jason had warned me that some colonies don't take well to humans and may look down on me even though I am the Luna.

I sit down eating now breakfast as Jason tells me everything. Both guardians and Alec will be in the room during the meeting but it doesn't make me feel any better. They can't do much of all of them decided to attack.

"Liz, talk to me."

I look up at Jason's concerned eyes. "I'm nervous. Some of them have never even seen a human and some have a strong hate for my . . . Kind."

Jason moves behind me, wrapping his arms around my waist. "You'll be beside me the whole time. You don't even have to say anything. Just, stay away from the Witches. They're a little crazy and have had a bad past with humans. The Vampire leader will be there and I know you'll want to rip off his head because of what happened to Rose, but you can't do that."

I mumble out a fine and Jason give me a kiss on the cheek.

"Everything will be just fine."

We arrive in a room with white tile floors and walls with marble pillars across the walls. At every pillar is a warrior from the pack because the meeting is taking place in the Werewolf colony.

A long rectangular black table fills the space which is already occupied with the council members.

The moment I enter the room, everyone heads snap in my direction. Some eyes widen, others sniff the air in my direction.

A girl around my age with razor sharp teeth gives a smile as if a predator has found its prey. Her eyes are almost black, her skin is white along with her hair that is tied back into a braid.

"Human." She says slowly, as if testing the word, savouring.

I avoid her gaze—everyone's gaze, as I follow Jason to our seats, with our guardians and Alec behind us.

We sit at the foot off the table, staring down at everyone's faces. I swallow heavily, feeling all their stares burn into me.

I feel Jason's hand land on my thigh reassuringly and I take a breath, ready to start this meeting.

"Alpha Jason, this must be the Luna."

I bring my head up meeting red, cold eyes and the pale skin of an older man. He has grey hair and I immediately know this is the Vampire Clans leader.

Jason gives a nod. "Yes, Rhazien. Everyone, this is the Luna and the newest member of this council."

"But she is a human." This comes from farther down the table from a handsome boy with brown hair and vibrant purple eyes. He doesn't look that much older than me but then again, this is a supernatural world, he could be immortal for all I know.

"Elwin, is there a problem with that?"

Elwin's eyes look towards me and I find myself entranced by him. "The faeries are more of a peaceful species but we haven't had the best past with humans." His voice is deep, low slow and graceful. He splays his arms out. "I think I can speak for all of us when none of us has had the best pasts with humans. But what do I know, I'm only a messenger at this meeting. Kalan couldn't make it."

The girl with predatory black eyes smiles and stares at me.

"I think it is quite interesting, don't you agree mother?" The women beside her are older but with more greyish looking hair. She smirks, looking towards me with those same eyes as her daughter. "I can hear here tiny, pathetic heartbeat. Oh, it's beating faster." Her sharp razor talon nails tap against the table.

Her eyes widen and I can hear a growl coming from Jason. "My mate has done nothing wrong and has caused no disturbance with your colonies and land. She is not like the other humans you have dealt with."

Rhazien laughs. His red eyes bore into mine. "I hope not, her human friend caused quite the . . . ruckus in my lands."

I feel my fists clench in anger and I try controlling my breathing. His kind took Rose, thinking she was me.

An older man at the back of the table with blonde hair and blue eyes who wears a green cloak looks up at me. "So there are two?"

Rhazien looks over at me with a menacing smile. "Well, only one now, the Vampires got quite excited hearing humans have crossed into our world and took a peek for themselves. It's been a while since they have tasted human blood. I guess they got a little too excited and drank her dry."

"Shame," The witch girl comments. "Humans can be quite the entertainment. Guess we're stuck with one now."

"Aurelia, *enough*," Jason says through Clenched teeth.

She smiles victoriously as if she's trying to get a reaction out of him.

By now, my nails are digging into the palm of my hands.

"My mate is now part of this council and you will accept that." Jason uses his Alpha voice and everyone slightly bows their heads, except for Aurelia.

"You know Ameria will not accept of this, Alpha Jason."

I can almost feel Jason tense beside me. The attitude of the room has changed and for the first time this meeting has started, I speak.

"Who's Ameria?"

Aurelia looks down at her nails. "Basically the leader of our whole world." She leans forward towards me and lowers her voice. "And she *hates* humans. She probably does know you're here, but I bet she's taking her time with you."

I feel sweat form in the palm of my hands and the enchanter at the end speaks up. "We do not speak so freely of her, *witch*."

Aurelia waves a dismissive hand. "And what will she do, kill us all? Then she won't have anyone to rule. Boohoo, someone doesn't like her, she knows." Aurelia turns her attention back to me. "Better protect that pathetic little heart of yours, Luna. If your mate hasn't told you, Ameria will come for you, it's only a matter of time. She does not accept your kind. Why do you think your Alpha has someone always guarding you and is so overprotective of you?"

This time Jason stands up, growling at her. "Enough!"

"He knows." Aurelia sings.

"I said enough!"

In the blink of an eye, Aurelia and her witch mother disappear into thin air, a trace of black drifting in the air.

14. NIGHTMARES

After the Witches disappeared into nothing, the council began having a hard time accepting a human. They kept saying how I was putting everything and everyone in danger with Ameria watching me.

"Who even is this women?" I ask as I sit down on the couch.

Jason sits beside me on the couch, run a hand through his hair. "We don't speak much of Ameria, but she's a cruel, powerful woman. She controls all our lands, watches all of us and my Colony hasn't had the best visits with her."

"What do you mean?"

"Ameria has had an . . . obsession with me, with my power and what my colony holds. And Ameria is always looking for more power. But now that I've found my mate who is a human— well let's just say she's not too happy."

"Why does she hate humans so much? Why does everyone seem to hate humans so much?"

"Now that is hard to answer. My colony hasn't had many dealings with humans in our colony. But apparently for Ameria, something happened a long time ago with humans and it's burned inside of her so deep that her hatred for humans never lessens but grows. No one really knows why she hates humans so much but whatever the reason, it must have been pretty bad."

"So this Ameria holds a grudge on my kind for something that happened a long time ago? She sounds real mature."

"Elizabeth," Jason grabs both of my hands, now sounding serious. "Ameria is dangerous, don't take her lightly. Aurelia was right about why I guard you so much: I am worried she will come here and take you away from me."

"Because I'm human."

Jason gives a nod and I take in a heavy breath. "She would have been after Rose too, only now she's a Vampire."

"So what, I wait here under the protection of guardians until she shows up on our doorstep?"

"No." Jason lets out a growl and pulls me into his arms. "She won't get close to our doorstep, not while I'm here with you. I won't let her touch you."

"She won't."

The sound of soft tapping had me sitting up in bed. I look over to see Jason sound asleep in bed.

I close my eyes again only to hear the soft tapping again. I gently move Jason's arm off of me as I open the door and stand into the hallway. I look to my left and right and surprisingly, the Guardians aren't there. I thought they were supposed to be outside our door.

I hear the tapping again but it's louder now and I go my left, following the noise.

I pass by a window, the moons light creating the only light source in the hallway.

Why is it so dark?

"Elizabeth."

The voice is like a whisper in my ear, but when I turn around, I see nothing behind me in the dark hallway.

"Elizabeth."

Again, but this time I can make it out as a soft female's voice.

I follow the voice down the hallway until I pass a door. Something in me beckons for me to open the door and I do, the wine of the door opening the only sound.

I walk into a dark room with only a single window, the moonlight casting the only light in this room.

The room is empty of furniture, the walls are bare.

"Elizabeth."

I turn to the left corner to see a dark figure move into the light the window casts.

The women is pale, her body skinny and slender, her black hair as dark as ash. Her eyes are all black, almost like bottomless pits.

"Hello, Elizabeth."

Up close, her voice sounds like it belongs to a snake.

"Who are you."

The woman tilts her head to the side, sliding a razor-sharp finger down the wall closest to her.

"Well, I guess I should tell you considering I do know you who are, human. My name is Ameria."

My eyes widen, my heartbeat beats faster and I can feel a cold sweat form on my forehead and on the palm of my hands.

This woman, this creature, whatever she is, is Ameria.

I swallow heavily backing up a step to the open door to get out of the room, but it slams shut, caging me like a mouse in a trap.

"Leaving so soon?"

My breathing becomes more intense as I feel the true fear of this women. She smiles at me reviling black, layer upon layer rows of sharp teeth. Ameria walks toward me slowly, gracefully, her moves silent. Her black slender dress, waving behind her almost like her clothes are made of shadow.

I find myself backing up only to stop abruptly, my feet almost like they are glued to the ground.

Ameria continues to walk to me as I'm forced to stay in my spot.

When she's about three feet in front of me, she tilts her head to the side. "You are so much more, tinier, weaker, then I imagined. Is all your kind like this?"

I keep my mouth shut and she laughs, walking closer to me until I have a full view of her face. I clench my hands into fists to stop them from shaking.

She walks around me, dragging her fingers across my shoulder and back feeling how sharp her nails are.

"You've caused quite the disturbance here in my lands, Elizabeth. You've kept *my* Alpha away from me. And I do not share my things."

I close my eyes shut, biting my lip hoping that she will just go away.

"I can hear your heart, your tiny, mortal heart beating under your skin. Such breakable skin."

My breaths come out ragged. Maybe if I scream someone will hear me. I open my mouth to scream but nothing comes out.

Ameria laughs. "No one will come to you here. Not while I'm here. I enjoy watching you squirm. I can smell the fear rolling off of you."

Ameria slides a slender finger down my arm, her nails grazing my skin. "You humans are always ruining things. My things."

Her nails suddenly dig into the skin on my arm and I wince in pain feeling hot liquid drip down my arm.

"Oh look at that, a quick little cut and you're already bleeding. So weak."

She faces in front of me, her black eyes searching my face.

She caresses my face with her nail as she smiles. "Now you listen, human. I've dealt with your kind before and you are nothing but a disturbance in my lands. You create chaos. I will give you two options because of how merciful I am."

Ameria holds up her index finger. "One, you leave immediately to your pathetic human world and never come again or two, you stay and I will come after you and everyone you love starting with that Vampire friend of yours. I don't care if you are the Luna, I will not have a human in my lands. And don't you worry about the Alpha. He will move on and I will take care of him. So think about it, you have three days to leave or there will be bloodshed."

I swallow heavily and at that moment she slashes her razor nails across my chest.

A scream erupts my throat and I suddenly sit up again in my room, with Jason holding me against him.

I stare around the room, realizing I'm back with Jason. He pulls away and the Guardians enter the room on guard staring at us and then sweeping the room with their eyes for the threat.

Jason looks back at the Guardians. "It's okay, she just had a nightmare." They nod their heads silently before retreating back into the hall.

Jason stars at me, caressing my cheek softly.

I look down at my chest to find it all intact. So that's what it was, just a nightmare.

"You okay?"

I can feel my hair cling to my skin as I nod. "It was just a nightmare," I say thinking that if I say it out loud it'll be more convincing.

But it felt so real.

"Do you want to talk about it?"

"It felt so real," Is all I say. My voice sounds hoarse as if I was screaming.

Jason tightens his arms around me. "It wasn't. This is real. And you scared the crap out of me, you just started screaming."

"I'm sorry."

"Don't apologize."

I find my eyes getting heavy as he holds me and I realize as long as I'm with him, I'm okay. Nothing bad will happen while I'm with him.

And with that, I repeat the same thought over and over in my head.

It was just a nightmare.

I wake up alone. No doubt Jason had to leave early to do some Alpha duties.

I get out of bed, feeling like the nightmare I had was all it was. Just a nightmare.

I make my way to the connected bathroom, stepping into the hot shower.

I should do some archery today. The last time I did archery was before I came here which has felt like forever.

After about ten minutes, I step out of the shower, wrapping a towel around me. I move to look into the mirror and stop in my tracks, my eyes wide.

Written in red on the mirror reads 3 days.

I scream.

It was just a nightmare. That's it.

A second later, the bathroom door opens and Ashley, my Guardian, comes running in, her black uniform a contrast against all the white.

She scans my body for any injuries before her eyes move to the mirror, taking in what's written on it.

3 days. Ameria said I had three days.

It's was just a nightmare.

Ashley stares at the mirror with wide eyes. "Are you okay, Luna?"

I nod, my hands shaking at my sides. It's was just a nightmare.

Ashley moves toward the mirror, sniffing it. Her eyes darken. "Its blood. I've mind-linked the Alpha and Beta. They're on their way."

I take a seat on the edge of the bathtub with my head in my hands.

It was a nightmare. I even woke up in Jason's arms. I never left the bed.

Nightmare. That's all it was, just a nightmare. But no matter how many times I repeat that in my head, the less I believe it.

15. 3 DAYS

3 days. That's all I had, whether the nightmare was real or not.

I sit on the edge of the bathtub when Jason comes running in towards me nuzzling his face in the crook on my neck, breathing in my scent.

Past him, I stare at the mirror, at the bloody words. Someone had come in and written those words.

Jason looks down to see I'm only wearing a towel wrapped around me and a growl comes out of him, his eyes going black, lustful.

Alec walks in the moment Jason grabs me by the wrist, out of the washroom.

Alec bows his head slightly as I pass. "Luna."

I give a quick smile. "Hey, Alec."

He smiles back as I'm pulled away and Jason opens the door to the walk-in-closest, bringing me inside with him.

He closes the door and brings his lips to mine, kissing me passionately. But it's not a soft, slow kiss, it's harder, faster, urgent, needed. He kisses me as if he'll lose me in any second or that he could.

3 days.

I pull away feeling a tear fall down my cheek.

Jason wipes it away with his thumb and kisses the spot gently. "Why are you crying."

I meet his eyes, his intense blue eyes and I shake my head. "I shouldn't have gotten close. I should have ran, I should have left. But I feel—connected to you. I've been trying to fight it, but I can't."

He might not know what I mean. I can't leave him, I can't do it. That nightmare with Ameria could have been fake but even if it is real, I can't do what she said despite the threat on my loved ones. Maybe if I tell him, he can help.

"You will never lose me."

I look back up at him, more tears falling down my face. "I can't stay here, Jason."

His eyebrows narrow together.

"My nightmare, it was about Ameria."

Jason suddenly goes very still.

"She trapped me in a room and I couldn't move. She told me that I have three days to leave her lands or she will hurt the ones I love and care about. 3 days before blood is shed."

Jason suddenly looks up at me. "3 days was written on your mirror."

I nod, feeling my stomach turn into a knot.

Jason runs a hand through his hair, his jaw clenched. "Liz, you didn't have a nightmare. Ameria was in your head, that was a message sent from her."

"Not a nightmare," I repeat.

Jason nods his head. "Ameria must have contacted you in your sleep, sending you a message and that dear, is very real."

Real. Not a nightmare, it was real, a message. She was inside of my head.

Jason brings up a hand to cup my cheek. "Breathe, Liz. Your heart rate is going crazy. I got you, Ameria will not come close to you or anyone here."

I point to my head. "She was inside of my head."

Jason nods. "You're human, it's easy for her to get into your head."

The thought of her being able to enter my mind, sending a message that feel so real makes my skin crawl.

"Jason, what do we do?"

Jason kisses both of my cheeks before looking at me. "Well, first of all, you are going to change because right now you are making it very difficult for me to keep my wolf at bay. Then you're going to have breakfast and do some archery to keep your mind off everything while Alec and I get my warriors together to plan something. You aren't leaving, Liz. Only if you truly want to. But you are safe here, don't let Ameria get to you."

I nod and his kisses my forehead. "Let's get some breakfast. While I'm gone Ashley will be with you."

We go down the stairs past the kitchen and living room and she opens a door revealing a room full of rows of different archery bows. On one wall are different types of arrows and arrowheads. On a table are different arm guards ad multiple gloves. I look over at the cage full of bows. It's amazing.

"Jason did this for me?"

Ashley nods. "He saw how much you loved it when he first saw you play. So he created a room for you."

Rose goes up to all the different arrows. "Damn, Liz. With all of this, you could kill an army."

I walk up to a crossbow hanging on the wall with a scope already attached. I've rarely ever used a crossbow.

Rose comes up beside me smiling. "You should try it out. Here, give me your bow, I'll hold it for you."

I hand Rose my bow as I take the black crossbow into my hands.

I reach the next door leading to outside where targets have already been set up for me. I breathe in the fall air, closing my eyes for a second. Rose and Ashley follow me behind as we walk into a slight clearing in the woods where targets have been set up for me.

I stand there, taking an arrow, and loading my crossbow. It feels like I haven't done this in forever.

Ashley and Rose stand a bit back, giving me room as I stare into the scope, at my target pinned up against a tree.

I take a breath, and fire, hitting close to the centre. I feel a smile forming on my face. I've missed this.

I reload an arrow looking into the scope to see Ameria standing there in front of the target. I look up, backing up in fear but she's no longer there.

Ashley and Rose move up beside me.

"Luna, are you okay?" Ashley asks.

I blink multiple times. "Yeah, I'm fine."

I look back into my scope seeing black flash before me and a cold laugh echo in my ears.

Stop, I wanted to say.

That cold, vicious laugh.

"Stop." This time I say it out loud and Rose steps up beside me. "What?"

The laugh comes again.

"I said stop!"

I shoot my arrow, missing the target completely, flying into the woods.

I breathe heavily as Ashley stands in from of me.

"Luna, you look pale. Are you sure you are alright?"

I stare off into the forest as if it's calling to me.

"Give me a second." I pass my crossbow into Ashley's hand as I walk off into the woods.

"Luna, I wouldn't—"

"I'll only be a second. Just wait here."

I jog out of the clearing and into the thick of the woods. The only sounds of my feet crunching leaves and sticks.

"Elizabeth."

My head snaps to my left to see Ameria leaning against a tree, arms crossed in front of her chest.

"What do you want?"

A cold, snake smile spreads across her face. "Such a bold question, human. But to answer your question, I realized you've completely ignored my order to leave."

I raise my chin. "I have three days."

"It doesn't sound like you'll be leaving at all. Not with that conversation you had with your Alpha Jason. I'm disappointed, I thought our conversations would stay in between us."

I clench my hands. "I'm not a fool. I will not accept being threatened and I certainly will not accept you threatening my loved ones. So if you think I am stupid and I will just walk away, think again. We humans, are stronger and smarter than you think. I would think you, Ameria would know better than to underestimate others."

Ameria snarls at me. "What's stupid is you not taking my merciful offer. Let's see if you will still be here in three days. You better have eyes everywhere here because no one can hide from me and no one speaks to me like that without consequences."

I feel a sharp stab in my chest and I'm soon flying back, my back hitting against a tree and falling flat on the ground, taking the breath out of me.

"Goodbye for now."

And then Ameria is gone.

I struggle for my lungs to take in the air. I flip onto my back bringing my hands to my chest. My shirt is covered in red, my blood and I struggle to breathe.

"Oh my God." I bring my hands to my chest feeling tears sting my eyes.

I let out a grunt in pain as I lean up against the tree.

I didn't realize how far I walked out into the forest when I see nothing but trees around me.

Great, just great. I'll die of blood loss before anyone will find me. I lift up my shirt to see big, red, deep, bloody claw marks. drop my shirt back down, resting my head against the tree. I close my eyes trying to calm my breathing. I press my hands against my wound, trying to slow down the bleeding.

"I'm okay," I say to myself.

I feel the world spin around me and my body begin to shake. It's getting darker now, colder and the sun is beginning to set.

I keep my eyes closed. I'm exhausted, so tired and exhausted. I feel a cold sweat form on the crown of my head and my breaths come short and ragged.

Despite everything that's happened, I find myself humming. A soft, melodic tune that I find myself soon falling asleep to.

My eyes open slowly. My body lays on the cold forest floor, shivering.

It's pitch black outside now and I can almost see my breath. I sit up against the tree, wincing as I look down at my bloodstained hands and clothes.

"I would have thought your mate would have found you by now." I know that voice. That cold, snake voice. I turn to my left, Ameria sitting on a tree stump, cleaning her nails.

"What do you want." I practically spit the words.

"Oh nothing, just admiring the view. I forgot how fragile you are."

"Bitch."

Ameria clicks her tongue. "Now, now, no need for such vulgar language."

"You did this." I spit blood to my side.

"Yes, I guess I did. It's not my fault you humans break like glass."

I snarl before I hear some movement to my left.

Ameria stands up and crouches before me. She presses her fingers into my wound, a scream escaping from me.

Ameria brings her bloody fingers to her nose, sniff my blood before licking her fingers. She then brings them away disappointed.

"Hmm, shame. I thought human blood tasted better."

She grips my chin suddenly and smiles, revealing her sharp teeth. "It's so easy to infiltrate your mind. It's like I'm tied to you when I do this." She then brings up her bloody fingers, my blood. "Bloody ties."

She then vanishes, as if the wind blew her away.

A moment later, I hear rustling to my left and a second later, multiple wolves jump out in front of me.

I scream, covering my head with my hands. If these wolves are rogues . . .

A minute later, I feel soft, gentle hands move mine down and my eyes meet Jason's dark blue eyes.

He's shirtless and only wears a pair of shorts.

He looks down at my chest, my bloody clothes and hands. A growl comes from him as the other wolves stand guard.

"Who did this?" His voice sounds deeper, more animalistic.

My breaths come out ragged and I feel tears sting my eyes. I'm a mess, a bloody mess.

I feel a tear fall down my cheek and Jason's face softens. He wipes the tear away, kissing my cheeks.

"You're okay, I got you."

I wince when I move forward.

"You're in pain. Can I?" His hands are on the ends of my shirt and I know he needs to check my chest.

I bite my lip and I nod. He gently lifts up my shirt and I hear his sharp intake of breath.

The world begins to spin around me and I shake my head leaning into Jason. "I don't feel good."

I feel fingers move to my neck. "Your pulse is slow, and you're pale."

"Liz?"

Past Jason, Rose stands there.

"I was so worried—"

She stops in her tracks staring at the blood on me, her eyes glowing red. "Blood."

I can hear her sniff the air and she stares at me as if a predator has found its prey.

"Guardians." One word from Jason and the guardians are in front of us grabbing Rose by the arms taking her away.

"Rose," It's merely a whisper but Jason moves so one arm is around my back and the back of my knees. He picks me up and begins jogging off with the wolves surrounding us.

"We need to take you to the doctors. Who did this to you."

I feel my vision move in and out of focus.

"Elizabeth, stay with me. Who did this?"

"Ameria."

16. HAUNTED

Darkness. Never ending darkness.

"Oh, Elizabeth."

No, not that voice.

You've got yourself in quite the conundrum."

"Get out of my head."

"You're mate is so terribly worried about you. But I won't let you wake up, not yet."

"What do you want?"

"You have two days left, Elizabeth. And on each day that you don't leave, something terrible will happen because of you."

"What did you do?"

"Oh and just like that, something happened."

"What did you do?" I repeat with urgency in my voice.

"You will find out soon enough. Reconsider your decision. You have two more days."

I find a sliver of light in the darkness and the call of my name.

I follow it until the light surrounds me and I find myself waking up to pain.

I open my eyes to light staring down at me and multiple faces.

"Elizabeth! Can you hear me?"

I turn to my side to see Jason, gripping my hand.

"Yes." My world swims around me.

"What happened?"

The doctors around me flash a light in my eyes.

You were attacked in the woods. You've lost too much blood. We need to do a blood transfer."

"I'll do it," Jason says immediately.

Jason," it's almost a whisper but he looks down at me caressing my cheek.

"You're okay," he says but I shake my head.

"No, no you don't understand. It's Ameria, she won't get out of my head."

I feel a doctor grab my arm to put the needle in but I pull it away.

"No, listen. You need to find a way to stop her from getting in my head. Something bad has happened. Where is everyone?"

Jason leans down and kisses me on the lips. "Everyone is okay. Focus on your breathing, you're panicking."

"Something isn't right, Jason."

"Just relax. You can't do anything when you're like this."

"No, Jason—"

I feel a prick in my arm and I look over at the doctor holding an empty syringe.

I feel a calmness talk over me, my muscles relax. My eyes even droop a little. A small smile forms on my face.

I feel another prick in my arm no doubt for the blood transfusion.

Jason kisses my hand. "Don't worry, Alec is looking over everyone right now. When we're done here, we'll go check on everyone."

I nod my head sleepily and I fall asleep into a deep slumber.

I wake up in my bed alone and right away, I know something is wrong. My Guardian, Ashley isn't here and neither is Jason, Alec, or Rose.

I look down at my bandaged chest before pushing the covers back and running towards the door. I whip the door open, stumbling into the hall.

Where is everyone?

"Hello?" I yell.

A minute later, I hear multiple footsteps running up to me, Jason, Rose and multiple guards.

Jason walks over to me and immediately embraces me. He puts his head in the crook of my neck breathing in my scent. "You're okay."

"I'm fine, Jason."

He moves away, looking into my eyes. I look past him to see Rose staring down at the ground, her face unreadable.

I move my attention back to Jason. "What's going on?"

Jason just shuts his eyes and shakes his head. "You were right."

I scrunch my eyebrows together. What was I right about? The only thing I said to Jason was that something terrible was going to happen, that—oh no.

"What happened?"

Jason looks at me as if trying to decide if he should tell me or not.

Jason, what happened?"

"It's Ashley, your Guardian."

I push past Jason and Rose, running down the stars. I run out of the house only to be met with Alec and about two dozen guards. Lying on the ground, pale and un-moving is Ashley.

"No."

I step forward but Alec puts an arm out cutting me off. "I'm sorry."

I feel tears burn my eyes. Ameria did this. She said that every day I don't leave something was going to happen, that someone was going to die.

My Guardian, my protector.

 I fall to my knees. "No!"

A minute later I feel strong arms surround me. I turn around to see Jason silently embracing me. I grip his shirt in my hands feeling tears streaming down my face.

I feel him rub soothing circles on my back and I breathe in his scent of the forest.

I did this. Her death is because of me. How many more will die because of me?

I feel anger take over. I feel it move under my skin like lava, waiting to erupt.

I move out of Jason grip to walk towards Ashley's body.

"Liz, I—"

It only takes a glimpse from me for Jason to close his mouth.

I move towards Ashley, kneeling beside her, not caring about the blood staining my clothes. Her face is so pale, the life gone from her.

I move a piece of her blonde hair out of her face, the ends soaked in blood.

Oh, Ashley.

I put my hands beside me, feeling her blood soak into my skin. I did this.

I bite my lip to stop more tears but fail miserably. I let out a silent cry as I put my forehead against her body.

"I'm so sorry."

I then sit there, crying, repeating those three words over and over.

I feel a tear of water hit my arm and I look up to see it has begun raining. Almost as if nature itself is mourning for the loss of her.

I shake my head. Ameria will pay.

I feel a hand land on my shoulder and I look up to see Jason looking down at me with sad eyes. I grip his hand as I look down at Ashley.

"I know who did this."

A growl comes from Jason. "Who?"

"Ameria."

"I know you probably don't want to think about it, Liz, but we need to find you another Guardian. You can pick if you want, but they need to have the training."

Jason, Alec and I are currently in his office, discussing what Ameria has been doing to me. It's almost dinner time and Jason has mentioned wanting to change my bandages.

"I don't want to talk about replacements right now."

I sit in a chair with my legs tucked in. Alec leaves the room silently as Jason moves towards me, kissing my forehead and tucking a strand of hair behind my ear."

"You look tired. Do you want anything to eat? I can make you something."

I shake my head. "I'm not hungry."

Jason kneels in front of me as another tear falls down my cheek. He moves forward kissing away the tear.

"I hate seeing you cry."

He then rests his forehead against mine. "We'll get through this, Liz. We're strong."

I shake my head looking up at him. "I want all of us to get through this."

17. GOLDEN EYES

I wake in the middle of the night covered in sweat, my muscles sore like I just ran a marathon.

Nausea rises and I throw the blankets back, push myself out of Jason's arms and I run to the bathroom, throwing myself against the toilet.

A second later, I feel Jason pull back my hair, rubbing my back in soothing circles.

I grip the toilet, the coldness soothing against the hear running through me.

When I feel like I'm done, I flush the toilet, keeping my head resting on the edge of it.

Jason goes to the counter grabbing an elastic band, tying my hair back into a bun for me.

He crouched down beside me, rubbing my back. "You're alright."

I lean into his touch, his arms soon wrapping around me.

A cold sweat runs down my back and the room tilts around me. "Jason, I don't feel good."

I feel nausea rise again and I push myself out of his arms and bring whatever else is in my stomach, into the toilet.

"I just mind-linked the pack doctor. He'll be here soon."

I don't even reply to him as I lean back, rubbing my stomach. What is happening to me?

Jason gently picks me up, putting me down on the edge of the bed.

"Let's get you into something comfier."

Jason disappears into the closet for a second before returning with one of his shirts and one on my PJ bottoms.

"Arms up."

I put my arms up as he grabs the hem of the shirt I'm wearing, all sweaty and gross, off of me.

I don't even care that he sees me in just a sports bra. He kisses my forehead before putting a black shirt on me. It's bigger and longer because it's his but it's still very comfortable.

"Is it okay if," Jason tugs on the pj's bottoms I currently wear, asking permission if he can take them off.

I give a silent nod as Jason gently pulls them off.

I can see his eyes turn slightly darker as he puts on a pair of shorts for me.

"Thank you," I mumble, feeling tired.

"Liz, stay awake, I want the doctor to check on you. He'll be here any minute."

My eyelids feel so heavy. Jason places his hands on either side of my face.

"Liz, open your eyes for me please."

I open my eyes, meeting his blue ones. His eyes widen in surprise and worry before his own eyes glaze over, no doubt mind linking someone.

A knock comes at the door to our bedroom and it opens to reveal Alec and Rose.

Alec moves to Jason's side, kneeling down in front of me.

"The doctor is on his way up."

I close my eyes only to be gently shaken by Jason.

"Stay awake, Liz."

Alec studies my face before turning to Jason. "No, I've never seen this before, Jason."

Rose moves to sit beside me, gripping my hand. "What's wrong with her?"

"We don't know," Jason replies.

Suddenly, a growl mixed with a whimper escapes my lips. Such an animalistic noise, I cover my mouth.

They all look at me wide-eyed before Jason's brother and Guardian, Thomas, walks into the room with the pack doctor behind him.

My body begins to heat up more, I can feel sweat drop down my forehead and back.

"Why is it so hot?" I begin to slowly fan myself as the doctor makes his way to me.

He flashes a light in my eyes and a look of shock forms. The doctor turns to Alec and Jason shaking his head.

Rose grabs my chin looking me in the eyes. She sucks in a breath.

"What is it?" I ask.

No one responds, all of them looking at each other.

I push myself off the bed, making my way to the mirror on the wall. My legs feel like jelly as I make my way, breathing heavy.

Why am I so tired?

"Liz, no—"

I ignore Jason as I stare in the mirror and I think my heart skipped a beat. My eyes, the outer ring now glows a golden yellow, like a wolf would.

"Oh my God." I fall to my knees, my head in my hands.

How is this happening?

Jason moves behind me, wrapping his arms around my shaking figure. "Liz—"

I turn around, facing him. "Is this Ameria? A trick to get me to leave? What-what is this? What is happening to me?"

I look up to the Doctor as he clears his throat. "I didn't think it was possible but, I think I might know what's wrong."

I wince as I feel a tightening in my muscles. Jason swiftly picks me up off the ground, gently laying me don back in bed.

"Now I may be wrong alpha but I think her body is rejecting the blood you gave her to save her. You're a werewolf, she's a human and her body is trying to adjust to the change. The blood is slowly changing some parts of her as a way of her trying to accept it, in this case, she's taking some of the traits of a wolf."

Suddenly, Jason's eyes become black, pitch black and his breathing intensifies. "I did this to her?"

His fists shake in rage as he tries to control his anger.

Alec steps forward, placing a hand on his shoulder. "Jason—"

A loud growl comes out of Jason as he runs out of the room. I feel a wave of nausea come over me and Alec quickly grabs me and runs me over to the toilet.

"Rose, can you get me a cold washcloth and a glass of water, please?"

Rose nods, leaving the room in the blink of an eye.

I lean against the toilet, heavily breathing. "Is Jason going to be okay?"

Alec's eyes soften and Thomas appears, leaning against the doorway.

Alec returns his eyes to me. "He'll be fine, he's just upset with himself, don't worry. Thomas, Rose and I will watch over you until he calms down."

"He can't get upset with himself over this."

Alec and Thomas move over to me, supporting me as I walk over back to the bed. They lay me down, Rose returning a second later, rolling up the facecloth and placing it on my forehead.

Alec draws the blanket over me. "He's the Alpha, Luna. The King of all Alphas and he can't stand the fact that he's causing you this pain."

"He saved me, Alec. Please, let him know that. I don't want him to be angry."

Alec slowly nods his head. Rose lays sits on the bed, her back against the headboard.

"Rose is going to stay with you here. Thomas will be outside your door and I'll talk to Jason. You just get some rest."

"Thank you."

Alec smiles. "You're my Luna. I'll do anything you need, it's an honour to be serving and protecting you."

With that, Thomas and Alec leave quietly as Rose passes me my glass of water.

"Did Ameria make another move yet? Is everyone okay?"

Rose nods. "Everyone's okay. Well, everyone except you. You know, in the morning while you get better, we should watch a movie or something."

I nod, grabbing her hand. "Sounds like a good idea. I miss us hanging out."

Rose's smile falters. "Me too."

I wake to Rose kneeling on the floor, going through movie dvds. I reach for the glass of water on the nightstand beside me, drinking it down greedily.

"Finally, you're awake. So I've chosen the movie we're watching. We're gonna watch The Hunger Games."

I rub my eyes as she gets the movie started. As she settles down beside me she looks me in the eyes.

"Still golden. It's kind of cool in a way actually."

I look at Rose's red eyes and now mine are changing gold. So much has changed to both of us, who we are and I can't tell if that's good or bad.

I just shrug my shoulders as she plays the movie. "My three days are up," I mutter.

"I know."

"Nothing has happened?" I ask.

"Not that I'm aware of. Have you heard from your mom?"

I look at my phone as I never thought much of it, but my mom hasn't tried contacting me in days.

"No, I haven't."

The last time I spoke with her, I came up with the excuse that I wasn't feeling well and Rose and I were staying a bit longer. I haven't heard from her since. Rose's mom has been worried sick about her daughter but Rose hasn't made any move to contact her and I don't blame her.

I think of my mom again. I know she would have tried contacting me. My stomach sinks as I realize. "Rose, I think I know what move Ameria made. I think she has my mom."

18. HALF OF YOU

I grab my phone, dialling my mom's number.

"Please pick up."

The phone continues to ring. "Pick up the phone, mom. Pick up the phone."

Rose paces the room, her own phone in her hand as she makes the choice to contact her mom. However, Rose's mom isn't picking up the phone either.

If this is Ameria's next move, to get to me and to now Rose, we have to go.

I lay in bed, my muscles still weak.

"Dammit!" Rose throws her phone at the nearest wall, it shattering to pieces with her new Vampire strength. "I purposely left so my mom wouldn't get hurt or involved in this supernatural world and now, Ameria could have them!"

"Rose—"

She whips her head in my direction, her eyes glowing red, her fangs extended and visible.

"Rose, you need to calm down."

I try moving towards her, only for my legs to crash down, me collapsing to the floor. I'm still weak.

"Thomas!"

Rose stalks towards me, like a predator approaching its prey.

I see her knees bend, a smirk growing on her face.

"Rose, no!"

She jumps towards me, a body colliding with hers in midair, taking her down to the floor.

Thomas is on top of her, holding her down, growling as Alec enters the room, moving towards me.

Alec picks me up, placing me down on the edge of the bed while grabbing my glass of water for me to drink.

"Are you okay?"

I nod, watching as Thomas leads Rose out of the room.

"I've mind-linked Jason."

"Alec, my mom and Rose's they haven't called in days and they aren't picking up the phone. They aren't answering our calls."

Alec's eyebrows furrow together. "What are you saying?"

"Ameria, she's made her next move."

Alec suddenly stands, his eyes glazing over before returning his attention back to me. "Your eyes . . ."

"I know, they're different now."

Alec shakes his head. "No, well yes they are but, they suit you. They're turning the same shade of blue as Jason's but they have a golden rim. The same gold Jason gets when he's in his wolf or when he allows his wolf to take control. You got a little bit of him in you now."

I feel heat rising to my cheeks as Alec disappears into the bathroom, returning with a hand-held mirror. "See for yourself."

I take the mirror, looking at myself and he's right. Not only that, but they are more vibrant, just like Jason's.

I smile to myself, handing Alec the mirror as Jason enters the room.

His black hair is ruffled a bit but besides that, there are no other signs of him being angry.

He looks at me, his gaze softening as he grabs my hands, kissing each of them.

"I'm sorry, Liz. I'm so sorry."

I shake my head.

A second later, Thomas appears at the door, looking panicked.

"Rose, she left, ran off towards the human colony."

My head turns to Jason. "She went to go find her mom."

Jason looks to Alec, no doubt being told by him what happened.

I'm surprised Rose left like that. She is obviously working off her anger right now but what I'm worried the most is how she's going to control her thirst when she's surrounded by so many humans.

"We need to go after her."

"You're still not feeling great, Liz. You need to rest."

Jason caresses my cheek and I hold his hand there.

"She can't control her thirst, Jason. Her anger alone made her lose control and if not for Thomas she would have gotten me. She's my best friend, I need to go after her. I can't stay here."

Jason grabs my hand giving it a squeeze. "Stand for me."

I get up on wobbly legs, falling into Jason's arms a second later. "I would take you with my Liz, but you can't even stand on your own two feet."

I rub my forehead, feeling frustrated. "I need to go. Rose and my mom need me."

"I'll go with Alec and I'll bring a couple of guards with me. We'll find your mom and Rose, okay? Thomas will stay here to protect you along with all my other guards. I'll call my sister and you two could hang out to pass time."

"But—"

Jason plants a kiss to my lips. "I know you want to come, Liz. I'll let Thomas know if I find anything. You just get better."

I put my head in my hands. Jason's right, I can't leave, not when I'm practically becoming half a werewolf.

"Fine. Be careful while Ameria's out there."

Jason, Alec and fifteen guards left right away to the human colony.

Thomas stands with me outside on the porch as I wave them goodbye, feeling an ache in my chest knowing Jason will be away for some time.

"Becca will be here by tonight so until then, is there anything you'd like to do?"

I just shake my head. "I think I'm actually just going to get more rest, I'm quite tired."

Thomas nods, a hands on my shoulders as he tries and supports me back to bed.

"If you need anything, I'll be right outside the door. I'll inform you when dinner is ready."

I nod, quickly falling asleep.

I wake up when Thomas brings me dinner and telling me Becca, Jason's sister has arrived.

She walks in behind Thomas, a smile on her face as she comes to see me.

"Thank you, Thomas."

He exits the room silently as Becca takes a seat beside me. "It's good to see you again, it's been a while. So how have you been?"

I blow out a breath, pointing to my eyes.

She laughs. "Yeah, Jason told me about that but I think it suits you. Your basically half Werewolf, half human. Kind of cool."

I shake my head. "I think Ameria—"

"No, no Liz. No talking of that bitch while I'm here. I'm fully aware of what's going on and Jason is dealing with it."

"You mean, this bitch?"

On the other side of the room, Ameria stands there, an evil cold smile on her face. My eyes widen, my heart pounding faster and faster.

"Thomas!" I yell but Ameria laughs.

"Oh, he's taking a nap right now."

A growl comes from Becca as she stands, claws extending.

Becca lunges for Ameria only to be frozen in spot.

Ameria looks at her disapprovingly before moving closer to me.

I stare in shock. "What have you done to my mom? To Rose's?"

Ameria walks along the room, glancing out the windows. "Oh, so you found out my next move. And don't worry, I did them a favour."

I feel my blood run cold. "What did you do?"

Ameria simply shrugs. "I found it so awful how you and Rose left your family like that, making them worry about you, so I wiped you from their minds since you so dearly want to stay here with your mate."

"You, what?"

Ameria smiles. "You heard me. I wonder what will happen when Rose arrives at home, only to find them clueless as to who she is. And then Rose's anger will rise and I wonder if she can control her thirst. Hopefully, Jason will get to her in time."

I sit on the bed, my limbs feeling numb. I put my head in my hands feeling tears fall down my cheeks.

"No."

"Yes. And this is the first of consequences since you decided to stay here when I told you to leave! I am Ameria, leader of all and you disobeyed me."

"No!"

I launch myself off the bed, running towards her only for her to disappear and to appear behind me.

One swipe of her hand in my direction and I fall to the floor, unable to move.

"You monster!"

Ameria smile and laughs before disappearing, leaving me on the floor as Becca unfreezes. I'm able to move again but I sit on the floor with my head in my hands, tears falling down my cheeks.

Becca kneels down beside me putting a comforting hand on my shoulder as Thomas bursts into the room.

"Liz, are you alright?"

I scream, an ear piercing, sad scream.

All of this because of me.

19. SHE IS QUEEN

Becca stayed there, rubbing my back as I leaned into her. Thomas told me that he mind-linked Jason letting him know everything that Ameria told me.

I shake my head. This can't be happening.

Tears continue to fall down my cheeks as I stand up grabbing my phone.

"Get out," I say it softly, hoping they'll respect my wishes.

"Liz—" Becca says.

"I said get out!"

Becca and Thomas leave the room silently as I sink to the floor, finding my moms number in my contacts. I press call hoping that Ameria is lying.

"Please pick up."

After the third ring, I hear my moms voice.

"Hello?"

I almost cry. "Mom, its Elizabeth."

Silence. "I think you have the wrong number."

I feel my heart break, my tears silently falling down my face. It takes all my strength to sound apologetic. "Oh, I'm sorry, I must have dialled the wrong number."

"Oh, okay. Goodbye then."

"Goodbye."

I sit there in silence for what feels like hours until I go into my voice message box, noticing that I missed a call from my mom and she left a message. I click play.

"Hey, Elizabeth, you must be at the archery tournament by now. I miss you so much! I hope everything is going well. Tell Rose I say hi. Give me a call back when you can. I love you."

I replay that message over and over until my anger takes over and I throw my phone across the room.

I lay flat on the ground, closing my eyes. No doubt Jason can feel what I'm feeling through the bond. But I just lay there, watching as the night takes over. I don't move. I just lay there until I finally fall asleep.

✦✦✦

I wake to someone shaking me.

"Liz, wake up."

I groan as I slowly open my eyes to meet Jason's.

Jason's eyes soften when he meets mine and a second later he's wrapping his arms around me, embracing me. I rest my forehead on his chest, staying silent.

I feel numb empty.

"You're back."

Jason slightly pulls away to look down at me. "Yes, I got back ten minutes ago."

"Is she . . ."

"We found her and we were able to bring her back sedated."

I shake my head. "I can't believe this happened. My mom doesn't remember me."

I feel a single tear slide down my cheek and Jason goes to wipe it away, kissing my cheek softly after. He rubs my back in soothing circles and I find my eyes beginning to get heavy.

"Liz?"

"Hmm?"

"I'm enacting protocol 45."

I move away slightly, my eyebrows drawing together in confusion.

"What's that?"

"I'm calling all the Alphas in my colony for a meeting. As King, I can take action against Ameria for what she's done and I plan on letting every single one of them know what Ameria has been doing, letting them know what she has become."

"But I thought she ruled these lands."

"She does. But I am a King, a King of Alphas, the strongest there is and I'm going to use that power to my advantage. I'm going to prepare my wolves for war. I'm going to send word to all the other colonies too and maybe we'll be given extra support. Ameria won't stop, so I'm going to make her stop."

"Jason, people could get hurt."

"Ameria is going to keep hurting you and everyone else if this continues. I already told Alec to prepare the meeting for tomorrow."

I nod, simply too tired to question him. But why should I? He is the King. He is power and strength. He knows what he's doing.

"How many are going to be coming?"

"There are eleven colonies so there will be eleven Alphas."

"And what's the population of your colony?"

"Our colony you mean. And to answer your question, there are one hundred thousand wolves."

My eyes widen. That's a lot of wolves.

Jason squeezes my hand reassuringly. "And Liz, I'd like you to be there. The alphas deserve to know there Queen."

I feel myself freeze.

Queen.

I'm a Queen of Alphas. The Queen of a colony.

I never even thought myself of that. I never thought I would have this much power, so much responsibility.

"I'll be there."

Jason smiles, kissing me on the forehead. "Thank you."

I run a hand through my hair, ready to fall asleep.

"How are you feeling? Have you gotten better?" Jason raises the back of his hand against my forehead.

"I've gotten better. I can actually walk and stand now for a bit."

Jason nods, staring into my eyes, no doubt trying to get used to them.

"Your eyes Liz, are beautiful."

I feel heat rise in my face and I turn away.

I feel an arm wrap around my waist and Jason lays us both down on the bed.

I lay my head on his chest closing my eyes and I fall asleep.

20. A SHEEP IN A PACK OF WOLVES

I draw the string of my bow back, concentrating, aiming at my target.

My mom doesn't remember me.

Breathe in.

Rose is sedated for almost revealing herself to the human colony.

Breathe out.

Ameria won't stop trying to get rid of me and hurting everyone I love and carry about.

Breathe in.

My arm shakes for holding the arrow back for so long and I let it go, the arrow flying way past my target.

I mentally curse myself as I hear Thomas laugh behind me.

As Jason currently searches for a suitable guardian for me, Jason has passed Thomas, his brother, his guardian to me for protection while Alec is with Jason.

I turn around, glaring at him.

"What are you laughing about?"

Thomas shakes his head as he walks towards me. "I thought you're good at this."

"I was. Maybe not anymore."

I lower my bow as Thomas clucks his tongue.

"Now no one told me you were one to quit and give up."

I stare at the target again and back to Thomas.

"Well now you know," I mumble as I walk back to the packhouse.

"Hey." Thomas grabs my wrist, Turing me around. "I know you've been through a lot, a lot is happening right now. But don't let this all get to you. That means Ameria wins."

I yank my wrist out of his grip. "I'm not going to let anyone else die because of me. If that means Ameria wins then so be it. My three days are up, it's only a matter of time before she makes her next move."

"So is that what you're going to do? Wait for her to make her next move?" Thomas snorts. "What about your move? What are you going to do?"

I throw my hands up in the air. "I don't know! I'm just a stupid human. A sheep in a pack of wolves. I'm useless."

Anger flashes in Thomas's eyes as he runs his hand through his hair. "You are anything but. You are our Luna, the Wolf colonies Queen. The Moon Goddess would not have paired you with Jason, my brother, The Alpha King, if you're not fit for the role."

"How can you say that?" I lower my voice, "when I've caused so much death and destruction. When war is on the horizon."

Thomas's eyes soften before wrapping his arms around me. He hugs me as my arms hang limp at my sides.

"Ameria has caused this. Not you, this is her doing. She just doesn't like how you're fighting back, not listening to her. And that, Liz, is the action of a Queen fighting for what she wants."

I walk down the hallway of the packhouse alone, making my way to see Rose.

Jason has been busy sending out news to all the alphas for the upcoming meeting. Becca is respecting my wishes to be alone and Thomas is letting me have a moment of alone time after I begged him for five minutes. In the meantime, I decided to visit Rose and see how she is doing.

I make my way down the hall, stopping in front on Rose's door. Two guards stand outside it and as I make my way to the doorknob, a guard moves in front of the door, blocking my way.

I raise an eyebrow at the guard. "Excuse me?"

"Sorry Luna, we have orders from the Alpha not to let you in until it is safe."

"I am the—"

"We know. But the Alpha does not want you inside until it is safe."

I cross my arms over my chest. "She is my friend. I want to go in there. I need to."

A loud crash is heard from the inside of the room, followed by the noise of glass shards scattering across the floor.

The moment both guards are distracted from the noise, I boot forward, grabbing the doorknob and opening the door.

Rose turns to me, pale, vicious, teeth baring.

Her eyes glow red and I feel anger boil underneath me.

"Why hasn't she been fed!"

Suddenly, both guards move forward, a worried, angered and urgent look in their eyes.

They move past me as Rose moves forward toward me, fangs bared. They grab her by the arms, a loud growl coming from both of them.

The one guard holds her arms behind her back as the other guard moves closer to me.

"The Alpha has been informed of her waking up. We didn't give her anything because she was still asleep. He'll be bringing up something for her."

A vicious growl comes out of the guard restraining Rose as she tries getting out of his hold.

I tear my eyes away from the sight, turning away.

I can't keep seeing her get like this. She can't keep losing control.

"I need some air. Let Jason know I'm out for a walk."

"Would you like—"

I shake my head. "No. I want to be alone."

I stayed out in the forest until the sun began to set. I had no doubt that Jason was wondering where I was but I needed space. I want to be alone.

Rose is a vampire, one who doesn't know how to control herself. And I don't blame her for she doesn't have anyone to help her. It's like becoming a wolf alone, trying to learn everything on her own.

For the first time, I realize how alone she could be. How she could feel.

I sit up in a tree, my legs dangling over the branch.

I watch the sunset, the colours spread across the sky. About a month ago, I didn't know this type of world existed.

Now I'm a sheep in a pack of wolves. No matter how high my ranking is, me being human changes everything.

I'm weak here and Ameria knows that.

As for Rose, I want to help her, but I don't know what to do and it breaks my heart seeing her like that.

And Jason, my Alpha, my mate, I can feel the bond getting stronger. Being away from him right now hurts and I just want him to wrap his arms around me. If I weren't human, we would be able to communicate mentally like he does with his pack.

Maybe I finally realize how lonely I've become, or in fact, how lonely Rose and I have both become.

I hear the crunch of leaves and sticks snap underneath me. I look down from the tree, seeing Ameria stand there, arms crossed, a smile on her face. Her black dress, almost as if darkness swirls around her, moves along behind her.

"We have some things to discuss."

I snarl, staying in my spot. "I'm not discussing anything with you. In fact, my Alpha will be coming any minute."

Ameria cocks her head to the side, her smile growling larger. "We all know that's a lie."

"What do you want?"

Ameria looks down at her sharp nails. "You. You're coming with me."

20. DISAPPEAR

"Me? You want me?"

Ameria lets out a cold laugh. "You denied my request to leave. Despite everything I have done to make you leave you still have not." She clicks her tongue and shakes her head. "Some Luna you are. Letting your friend die and become a vampire, your own guardian, what was her name? Ashley? You let her die. And then you and Rose's family forget who you are. And yet, you still stay."

The air shifts, becoming tenser. Ameria's expression changes to a scowl. "No one denies me and now you are to pay the price."

She flicks her wrist and I fall from the branch I was sitting on and I fall to the ground.

I land on my side before Ameria, my side crying out in pain and I bite my lip.

I know Jason would have felt that through the bond. He must have.

I spit at Ameria's feet. "Jason is going to kill you. He will hunt you down if you take me."

Ameria shrugs her shoulders. "Let him. He won't find me."

If Jason is on his way, he needs to know where I am.

So I scream.

But nothing comes. Nothing but air rushing out of my mouth.

I snarl at Ameria as she laughs.

"Silly human."

I get up on my feet. "You're not taking me."

I turn on my heel, running.

I have no clue where I'm going but it's away from her.

Her laugh echoes behind me and I turn to try and find her. Nothing but the forest surrounds me and when I turn around again she stands right in front of me.

Her cold, slender hand wraps around my wrist and before I can pull it away, night sky wraps around me.

I stumble forward landing on my knees.

The ground is dirt and dead weeds, the night sky missing the stars. Trees bare of leaves surround the area and in front of me is a grey mansion.

Torch lights light the path to the building and when I look closer, I notice they are made of bones.

My blood seems to run cold and I stay frozen in my spot as two creatures come walking toward us on their hind legs.

Their skin is green and slimy, their eyes black, claws sharp enough to rip someone's throw out.

Ameria brushes beside me, walking towards the mansion as both creatures come towards me.

Oh hell no.

I get up onto my feet, adrenaline pumping into my veins.

If they're going to take me, I'm going to make sure to make their job a living hell.

But I can't do anything. Ameria just waves her hand in their air and I collapse to the ground, darkness surrounding me.

I wake on a cold concrete floor surrounded by darkness.

No lights are on. I'm surrounded by four concrete walls with one single metal door.

My head throbs and my bones ache all over.

How long was I out for?

I get around and pace the room, looking at all the corners, searching for something that could help me escape. But the walls are bare.

A distant bloodcurdling scream has my head snapping towards the door.

My breathing gets faster and my hands turn to fists, shaking.

True fear begins to take over as I find myself frantically searching the room for an escape.

I keep moving around in the room, unable to sit still.

There's always a way out. Always.

Another scream.

I sit, my hands covering my ears and I rock back and forth. I don't know how long I stay in the position but the door opens, my head snapping up hearing the creak of the door.

Ameria walks in with a smile on her face with two of those creatures behind her.

I get up to my feet, meeting her cold gaze.

Don't look away, don't back down.

"You think you're so tough. You think you can outsmart me. You think you can disobey me. Well, you are wrong."

I back up as she comes into the room.

"Very wrong."

21. TRIALS

I don't know how long it's been. I don't know if it's day or night, today or tomorrow.

I lay on the floor, surrounded by darkness, waiting. For what exactly, I don't know. To be saved or to be killed.

The screams seem louder and I do my best to block them out. But it still makes me jump.

At one point though, the door opens, and a tall, handsome man with brown hair and green eyes walks in.

I quickly stand, my hands in fists. I glare at him, watching every move he takes towards me. I step back every time he does but my back soon hits the back of the wall.

The man stops moving towards me and he narrows his eyes at me. "So this is what a human looks like." His voice is deep, smooth.

I notice the crossbow strapped across his back and the dagger sheath on the side of his thigh.

"It's rude to stare."

The man looks around the room and then back to me. "And I don't care."

"What do you want?"

The man laughs. "The lovely Ameria would like to see you."

I sit on the floor. "Well, I don't."

He tilts his head to the side, an amused smirk growing on his face. "I wasn't asking."

"And I'm not going."

"You would think having an opportunity to leave this room would benefit you. Hearing all those screams all the time must get on your nerves by now."

He's right about that, but I will not see her. I'd rather be surrounded by darkness than to deal with darkness itself.

So I stay silent and move my attention to the ground. I hear footsteps move closer towards me and I see the man crouch down in front of me.

"I guess you're going to make my life as difficult as possible now aren't you?"

I keep my gaze trained on the floor.

"You're making this worse for you. Either you come willingly or I force you."

I look up at him this time and I notice his ears are pointed. He's not a werewolf, his eyes aren't red so he's not a vampire either. Witches are a little insane and their skin is more on the pale side.

"What are you?"

The man smiles and grabs me, throwing me over his shoulder as he walks out.

The halls are stone and are lit with torches. More of those creatures line the wall.

We arrive in a large room a split second later. Almost as if we used super speed.

The man dumps me onto the ground and I fall onto my knees.

The room is large with stone walls and floors. A red rug from where I kneel to the throne Ameria sits on is the only colour. Those creatures and people in white robes line the walls of the room.

Ameria sits in a black gown, staring bored at her sharp painted red nails.

"Aiwin, I see you were having some difficulty with the human."

So that's his name. I look up at the man beside me and he merely nods.

Aiwin makes his way to stand beside Ameria's throne, his hands behind his back standing tall.

He can't be much older than me. He looks young and so Ameria must have gotten him young.

Ameria turns her attention to me. I feel my own blood run cold and the hairs on the back of my neck stand.

I stand on my two feet, glaring at Ameria.

Ameria taps her nails against the armrest of her throne. "Weak, aren't they?"

No one in the room responds as Ameria stands up. "Humans are so fragile."

She spreads her arms out, looking at everyone. "Everyone take a long look for this," she points a finger at me. "Is a human! Weak and pathetic."

I scoff, anger boiling under my skin.

"She thinks she can outsmart me. She came to this supernatural world without permission, she's an intruder. I show mercy, giving her three days to leave and even when things begin happening to those she loves, she stays! All because of an Alpha King. Her mate."

The room stays silent and I grit my teeth together to stay silent.

"She didn't leave this world when I asked and now she must face a punishment."

Ameria circles me before stopping in front of me. "I have come to a decision. Your punishment will be The Trials."

Aiwin's head snaps up into my direction as Ameria makes her way to the throne.

"There will be three trials, obstacles you must survive and if you do, then you will leave this world unless the Alpha changes his mind on your . . . Mortality and if that changes, then you can stay."

So if I pass the trials she gives me I either leave this world, leave my mate unless I become an immortal. Or I die during my trails and I don't survive.

"It will start tomorrow. Aiwin, put her back where she belongs."

Aiwin grabs me by the arm and leads me back to my cell practically throwing me on the ground. He doesn't leave immediately though. He slams the door shut, trapping us both inside as he runs a hand through his hair.

"Dammit." I hear him mutter under his breath.

I sit on the floor, looking up at him.

He looks down at me, his gaze hard. "Get through the trials." With that, he leaves.

"Yeah, no shit," I mutter.

JASON

"We have no leads." I punch the wall next to me in anger as Alec tells me this.

"She's been gone for over twenty-four hours now and I—I can't feel her through the bond."

"We won't stop looking, you know that."

I take a seat in a chair. I'm exhausted. With Liz not here, I've been falling apart.

"When are the Alphas coming?"

"Tomorrow."

I stand, looking out the window. "Good, because they better be ready to discuss a war."

22. BARGAIN

I wake up with my muscles hurting, everywhere is sore from

the hard floor I've been forced to lay on.

I've been living off of bread and water for who knows how long and I've been waiting for my first trial.

Aiwin hasn't come to get me but his behaviour is . . . Strange. He told me to win but why? Wouldn't he want me dead?

I run my hands on my face as I try getting did of my grogginess.

I miss Jason. I miss being held by him. And maybe it's the bond making this way but I need him.

I've walked every space of this room, I've looked in every corner, every crevice as I tried looking for any way to escape to no avail.

I don't know how Rose is either. Ever since she's become a vampire I've rarely seen her because of her struggle to control her thirst.

I lean against the wall rubbing my face with my hands. I'm so used to the darkness, I haven't seen the sky or felt the sun on my skin in so long. Who knew I'd take that for granted.

I still haven't gotten used to the screams and maybe Aiwin was right. Maybe going to see Ameria has become a blessing.

I sink to the ground, wrapping my arms around me. An ache in my chest begins to grow and tears burn my eyes but I don't let them fall. No, I am stronger that. Ameria will not break me.

JASON

"Are they all here?" I ask.

Alec stands beside me outside the packhouse while black SUV's drive up the road toward us. All the alphas in my colony are coming in regards to their king. To me.

"Yes. They are all on time."

I nod. Ever since Liz has left I haven't stopped looking or trying to find leads. My scouts and warriors have been working around the clock for their Queen but we've found nothing.

Nothing, like she's just disappeared. A human lost in a supernatural world.

Alec gives me a side glance.

"We'll find her."

"We need to work faster."

Alec faces me. "And you need sleep."

The SUV's stop in front of us as Alec moves to stand next to me again.

"And I need my mate."

The doors open as countless Alphas come out of the cars, some with their mates.

The first one to walk up to me is Ethan, Alpha of the Shadows pack.

"Your Majesty, an honour to be seeing you."

"It's been a while, Ethan. Please, one of the maids will take your things for you. You know where to go."

Ethan nods, moving along as other Alphas come to meet me.

It's been a while since I've had to call a meeting like this and they all know why.

"Something's not right," Thomas says as he walks up to my side as the last Alpha walks inside.

I'm about to open my mouth when Thomas, my guardian, grabs the last Alpha who came to meet me, Ryan, by the collar of his shirt.

A growl escapes Thomas's mouth and Ryan's eyes suddenly glow purple.

"Glamour." Thomas snarls.

I narrow my eyes at Ryan and a smirk forms on his lips and a feminine laugh escapes his mouth.

"Witch." I snarl.

The glamour falls and there stands Aurelia, the witch from the council who told us about Ameria coming after us.

Her black hair is pulled back into a braid, a blood red cloak covers her body along with multiple weapons on her waist.

Her eyes glow purple before turning black letting us know she's not using her magic anymore.

"I must say, I thought you began slacking there. You almost let me right into this wonderful home."

Thomas grips her by the arms which must hurt her but she doesn't flinch.

"I hear your previous Queen has gone missing. I do remember saying something along the lines of, Ameria will come for her."

"What do you want? You're intruding wolf colony."

Her cold, black eyes meet mine. "Would you believe me when I say I come representing the aid of the witch colony? We'd like to help."

I scoff. "Stop wasting my time."

"It's true. We witches have had enough of her rule."

"You witches never do somethings without something back."

Aurelia shrugs. "True. But I guess this will decide how desperate you are."

"Only a fool would make a deal with Witches." I begin to turn away.

"A fool would reject the opportunity of more help to find their Queen."

I pause, my jaw clenching. "What is your price?"

Alec is beside me in a second. "I strongly suggest you don't—"

I hold up my hand silencing him. I turn to Aurelia and motion for Thomas to let go of her. After a second, he hesitantly let's go.

Aurelia wears a smug expression on her face. "We will give you myself and my best team of fighters for in return, we wish for one tiny thing. After Ameria is taken down someone will need to rule.

The Witch colony wishes to do so. That is our price."

23. MONSTERS

I wake to someone nudging my side. I look up in my daze to see Aiwin nudging me with his foot to wake me up.

"About time," he mutters as he sees me wake up.

I groan as I feel how sore I am from lying down on the hard ground.

"It's time."

I look up at Aiwin. I know exactly what he's talking about. These damn trials that Ameria wants me to do.

I feel a knot form in my stomach, a burst of nervousness form. I stand up, blowing out a heavy breath.

I'm not ready for this. I barely know how to fight. All I know is how to shoot arrows.

Aiwin leads the way out of my cell back into Ameria's throne room.

She sits casually there in her long black dress that frames her pale frame. She wears blood red lipstick and smiles at me as I'm forced to kneel before her.

Aiwin takes his spot beside Ameria with his arms behind him, standing tall. His crossbow is still attached to his back with daggers sheathed on the side of his legs.

He's a warrior.

"I think you deserve some fun after being cooped up in that cell."

A lizard-like creature throws something in front of me. The thud the only audible noise in the room.

It's a black bow.

A second later a quiver filled with black arrows lands in front of me.

I don't touch either of the items. I get a bad feeling off of them by just staring at them.

"What is this?" I ask.

Ameria pouts. "A bow and arrows. I heard you are quite good. I thought you would have been happy with my gift."

"If it came from you it must be made by hell itself."

Ameria laughs and then stands. "Those are your weapons for today's trial."

I raise an eyebrow as I look down at the weapons in disgust.

Ameria walks towards me and bends down to pick up the bow. She runs her fingers along the curve of the bow before throwing it towards me.

"Trial one: The hunt."

I furrow my brows in confusion.

"I'm sure we are all curious to see how well a human can fight. Kill three of my prisoners and you'll live for trial two. Be quick and careful or they'll kill you first."

I open my mouth to say something but Ameria snaps her fingers and the room dissolves around me, replaced with barren trees around me.

The quiver is now attached to my back, the bow in my hand.

It's night time, the sky pitch black. It's quiet, no noise heard except for my steps.

"Kill three prisoners," I mutter to myself.

Kill. I can't do that. I can't take three lives. I've never taken a life.

What was Ameria trying to prove? That I'm a monster and kill innocents? That humans are horrible creatures?

I shake my head as I load an arrow into my bow. What other options do I have? It's either kill or be killed. Was I prepared to take a life? Three? No, I'm not.

I shut my eyes to collect my thoughts. I have to do this.

A twig snapping to my right has me opening my eyes and me turning in that direction.

I would be lying to myself if I wasn't scared. I can't see anything around me. I'm going blind here practically. I need to focus on my hearing.

I hear the crunch of leaves behind me and I turn, releasing my arrow in that direction.

I hear a sharp intake of a breath before a thud. I move slowly in that direction before my foot hits something.

I look down to see a body, a young girl, with an arrow in her stomach.

A pool of blood surrounds her. She's still, not breathing, dead.

I killed her.

I put a hand to my mouth to avoid a cry escaping. She almost looks my age. I killed her.

All those who loved her, who will never see her again.

I killed her.

Without hesitation, out of fear.

I killed her.

"I'm sorry," I mutter.

I hear footsteps and I snap my head in that direction. I go to grab an arrow but I stop, looking down at the girl dead at my feet.

I can't do this.

My breaths become heavy, the footsteps get closer.

I grab the arrow, pulling the string back, aiming in the direction where the footsteps are coming.

Please stop coming towards me. Please.

But they come closer and closer. Not knowing what awaits them.

Don't make me do this.

I glimpse down at the girl dead on the ground.

Don't think about it. Don't think.

Suddenly, a male is shouting, coming straight for me with a knife in his hand. I act on instinct to protect myself and I let the arrow fly.

It lands in his throats and he drops the knife before his knees hit the ground.

He claws at his throat as blood seeps out. His eyes wild, staring at me before he drops to the ground dead.

My whole body shakes and I drop the bow. I feel numb as I stare at the two bodies at my feet.

I can't do this.

I'm done.

I kneel down on the ground letting a cry escape my lips.

I don't know how long I stayed there until I heard the crunch of leaves, the pounding of feet running towards me.

No.

Before I can grab my bow, a body collides with mine and I land in the pool of blood from the girl beside me.

A man straddles me by my waist and without thinking, I bring my legs up, caging his neck and I squeeze my thighs cutting off his air supply.

I feel him claw at my legs, for me to release but I keep the pressure on. He grabs a rock and throws it towards me causing me to release my hold on him.

I roll to my side moving away from him. But he grabs my legs dragging me back. I claw at the ground and I notice my quiver full of arrows. I reach my hand out for one, the end of an arrow just touching my fingertips.

Just a little further.

I bring my elbow back and I smash it into the guys face. He let's go of my legs, his hand going to his face as he screams in pain.

I use the opportunity and I grab an arrow. I roll onto my back and I stab it into his side. He doubles over, falling to the ground.

I get up into my two feet as I grab another arrow and my bow.

I aim and fire, the arrow finding a home in his heart.

I breathe heavily as silence fills the air. Three bodies surround me, sticky blood covers my skin and clothes.

What have I done?

I close my eyes, but I can still see their faces.

My hands shake and I try rubbing the blood off of me.

Suddenly, my surroundings melt away and I'm back in the throne room where Ameria sits.

Aiwin looks at me holding an unknown emotion in his eyes.

I kneel on the ground covered in dirt and blood and I stare at the ground.

I had to do it. I had to.

I hear clapping and it snaps me out of my thoughts. I look up to see Ameria standing, clapping as she walks her way towards me.

"Now *that* was entertaining."

I clench my fists and I shake my head. "I killed them. All three of them."

"Yes, you did."

"Why did you make me do that?"

Ameria grips my chin and forces me to look into her eyes. "Because in this world we are all monsters. And if you want to stay, you need to become one too."

24. TO BECOME

I kneel before Ameria, staring up into her cold eyes. This woman made me kill three people so that I would become a monster, a killer.

This world is full of monsters, but so was my world, the human world: murders, criminals. I didn't need to become that.

"Well done human."

I clench my hands into fists as Ameria turns back to her throne.

I still have my bow in my hand and the quiver on my back. So without thinking, with Ameria's back to me, I act quickly.

I take an arrow, drawing the bows string back, aiming at Ameria.

I release the string and the arrow goes flying in the air but it stops right before Ameria.

Her cold laugh echoes throughout the room as she turns around, the arrow turning to black dust.

"You think you can kill me with that arrow? I made those weapons with my magic, fool."

I stand on my two feet as Ameria snarls at me.

"You should know better than to give a weapon to a monster."

"Aiwin, deal with our guest. She seems to lack in manners."

Aiwin moves towards me but I glare daggers at him.

"Touch me and I'll kill you."

Aiwin smirks as he continues to walk towards me. "I'd like to see you try."

He grabs me by my arm dragging me out of the room.

We walk a few feet away before he throws me onto the wall, grabbing a dagger at his side.

"That was stupid of you."

I eye the dagger in his hand before meeting his eyes.

He holds his intense gaze with mine before another emotion flashes before his eyes and disappears as quickly as it came.

He then thrusts the dagger towards me and I scream.

The knife lands right beside my head and I have to blink a couple times to realize I'm okay.

Aiwin takes the dagger and sheaths it back in the pocket of his thigh.

He then grabs me by the arm and brings me back to my cell before running a hand through his hair.

"Why did you do that?"

Aiwin snaps out of his thoughts and looks down at me.

"Ameria wanted me to punish you and she'd want to hear proof of me hurting you."

I stare at him confused. Why wouldn't he hurt me? Why wouldn't he follow Ameria's orders?

"Why didn't you just hurt me?"

"I can't."

I raise an eyebrow in question.

Aiwin rolls his eyes. "You wouldn't understand."

And then he was gone, leaving me in my dark cell alone.

I curl up into a ball on the floor realizing now what I've done. Letting my actions sink in.

I killed three people.

I am a monster.

JASON

I stare at Aurelia for a couple seconds before I laugh. In order for me to receive help from the Witches, to save my mate and the whole supernatural world, they want to be the rulers after Ameria is dead.

I open my mouth to say something but Alec beats me to it.

"Hell no. Do you think we're stupid?"

Aurelia shrugs. "No, but I do think you are desperate."

I cut in before Alec can say anything. "I just had every single Alpha in my colony come here. You couldn't possibly help us anymore."

I turn on my heels with Alec right behind me.

I'm just about to enter the packhouse when Aurelia speaks up.

"My fellow Witches may not be able to offer much more power but I can."

I turn, anger rising. "What could you offer?"

An amused smirk forms on Aurelia's face. "Well, would it help you to know that I know where Ameria is?"

I stand there shocked and Alec growls.

"How dare you play such games."

Aurelia's smirk doesn't fall. "It's true. I know where your Queen is."

I march towards Aurelia grabbing her by the front of her cloak.

"Where is she?" I growl. She knows where Liz is, where my mate is.

Aurelia keeps her mouth sealed and I throw her to the ground as anger boils underneath my skin.

"WHERE IS SHE?"

"Jason."

I turn towards Alec where behind him all the Alphas stand.

I close my eyes. I need to calm myself. My wolf is losing control.

"Tell me now, Witch."

Aurelia stays on the ground looking up at me. "I don't say anything until we have a deal, Dog."

Aurelia is the only lead we have on Liz. We have nothing. Nowhere to go or look.

I turn to look at Alec who looks just as defeated and he nods at me.

"If I make this deal with you, I get your best warriors and all your information of Ameria and where my mate is."

"Yes, and in return, we will be the colony that rules."

I shut my eyes. This is the only way.

"Deal."

25. DAUGHTER

ELIZABETH

I lay on the cold floor alone. I don't know how long it's been since Ameria has taken me away but the urge to see my mate, to be in his presence has begun to drive me mad.

I'm angry.

I hate Ameria and every person, creature here.

Another scream but I don't jump. I've gotten used to that here.

The door to my cell creaks open and I lift my head to see Aiwin step into the room.

He's like Ameria's dog. Where ever she throws a stick he will go.

"Ameria demands your presence. Let's go."

I continue to lay on the floor staring at the ceiling.

"Did you not hear me?"

This time I sit up, staring up at him. "Oh, I heard you."

Aiwin's eyebrows draw together confused.

"Then get your ass off the floor."

I look past Aiwin. It's been days, weeks maybe since I've seen the sun, felt the breeze hit my skin, felt Jason's lips on mine, his touch. I've been surrounded by darkness for so long. This isn't living, I can't keep doing this.

Every time I sit here I still feel the blood on my hands of the three lives I've taken. Ameria took the memories of those I love away so there's no one else.

I can't keep doing this. I'd rather be dead.

"Elizabeth."

I snap my head up to Aiwin who now kneels before me, an arm on my shoulder.

"Kill me," I whisper.

Aiwin draws his hand back.

"Kill me!"

Aiwin just kneels there, a pained expression forming on his face.

I fist my hair on the sides of my head repeating over and over.

"Kill me, please."

Aiwin stands but I grab onto the front of his shirt.

"Please!"

Tears stream down my face, my voice is weak, dead.

Aiwin surprisingly places gentle hands on top of mine and kneels back down on the ground.

Aiwin stares at me right in the eyes and his begin to glow green.

"Elizabeth, breathe." His voice seems to echo in my brain. It's calming, reassuring.

"You are okay."

My surroundings seem to melt around me, the darkness disappearing replacing with sunlight.

The stone cold floor is replaced with grass.

He places the palm of his hand on my cheek.

"Everything will be okay."

Slowly, my surroundings return and I'm back in the cell.

Aiwin stands, grabbing me by the arm to lift me back onto my two feet.

"Ameria demands to see you. You have to see her."

My breathing evens out and I rub my sweaty hands on my pants.

"I don't understand," I mumble.

The edges of Aiwin's lips turn up for a second revealing a soft smile. A part of him I've never seen before.

"Come on." Aiwin ushers me out and just like that, I'm brought back to this living hell.

We enter the throne room but this time it's filled with people. Witches.

Ameria is casually sitting in her throne with a glass in her hand filled with red liquid.

Aiwin nods towards her in greeting and Ameria's cold eyes meet mine.

She smiles and stands, lifting her glass in the air.

"Ah and here is what we've all been waiting for!" Ameria then lifts her glass in my direction. "This is the human! The mate to Alpha Jason, Luna and Queen of the Wolf Colony."

Ameria's voice seems to cut through the air at the end creating a tense scene.

"A pathetic human."

Ameria snarls and all the Witches stare at me, circling around me, whispering to each other.

I glare at each and every one of them.

I am not afraid.

I am not scared.

But no matter what I tell myself, I am scared. My legs feel like jello, my hands shake, my heart beats like it's ready to fall out of my chest.

I have no one to help me, to protect or aid me.

Jason isn't here. Rose isn't here. or Alec, or Thomas.

I'm all alone.

The silence is ended by the click of heels coming from behind me.

We all turn around and I see a slim hooded figure making their way towards us.

Their cloak is red and their hood covers their whole face.

The person stops not too far away and pulls the hood down with pale hands.

The black hair, black cold eyes, evil smile.

"Everyone," Ameria snaps our attention to her as we then look back at the woman who entered the room. "This is my daughter, Aurelia."

I stand shocked. Aurelia, the Witch at the council meeting, who spoke and brought up Ameria first, who showed no fear of her.

Aurelia makes her way towards Ameria who sits on her throne. Her red cloak flows behind her.

Aurelia stops in front of me. "Well, well. So wonderful to see you again."

She brushes past me up the few steps to Ameria's throne.

"Mother," she acknowledges.

She stands to her right side as Aiwin stands on Ameria's left.

I knew we couldn't trust these damn Witches. But what are they doing here?

Ameria taps her armrest with her nails and rests her chin on her hand on the other armrest.

"We are in need of some entertainment and I thought, what could be better than the human I have here completing her second trial!"

The Witches all hoot and cheer as Ameria glares at me.

I feel my shoulders sag. I'm not ready for this trial.

Ameria snaps her fingers and three pedestals stand before me.

The left pedestal holds a dagger, the middle a stake, and the right a sword.

I look at the weapons and then back to Ameria.

A smile forms on her face.

"Pick your weapon."

26. PUPPET

I stare at all three weapons. A dagger, a stake and a sword before looking back up at Ameria.

I flash back to what I did to those three people, in the first trial.

I step away shaking my head.

"No."

Ameria tilts her head to the side amused.

Three people are ushered into the room and kneeled before me. Two men and a woman.

I stare at each and every one of them before looking up at Ameria.

"I don't care what you say, you will do what I say. Now pick a weapon."

I just stand there, staring at Ameria and then Aurelia.

Pain explodes behind my eyes and I sudden scream erupts from me. I fall to my knees, my legs weak.

It feels like my mind is on fire, like my mind is slowly becoming mush.

I clench my head, my vision becomes blurry.

"Stop," I croak out.

The pain intensifies.

"Stop!"

The pain ends and soon the room is filled with Ameria's laughter.

My ears ring, my legs feel numb and my whole body shakes.

I look up at Ameria as she smiles down at me.

"Pick a weapon."

I grit my teeth and fist my hands. Of course, she would force me to do this.

Angrily, I grab the dagger and the other two pedestals disappear.

"Your task is simple. Each and every one of these people before you are criminals. However, you humans seem to be so merciful so you can keep two alive but one of them must die."

I take a step back from them. I can't do this, not since my last task. I'm still haunted by the three lives I had to take. And now I have to take another one. I can't do this, not when I can look them in the eyes and watch the life drain from one of them.

I look down at the dagger I'm holding. My breathing intensifies.

I can't do this.

I can't.

"I knew you wouldn't be able to do it. Pathetic."

My body suddenly feels like a puppet on strings. My bones tense, my body shakes.

Aurelia's hand dances in the air, black magic following behind. An amused smirk forms on her face.

My left leg steps forward, then my right. My hands clenched tighter on the dagger.

No.

No, no, no.

I try to stop moving, I did my heels deeper into the ground but Aurelia's hand turns into a fist and I step forward again towards the man kneeling before me.

"Please," my voice is weak as I beg to Aurelia. "Please don't make me do this."

I step closer to the male kneeling before me. He stares up into my eyes as I make my way closer to him.

"Aurelia," I beg again but her smirk grows bigger.

She's controlling me with her magic, I can't do anything but watch my actions. She's gonna make me kill this man.

My arms and legs shake as I try to stop myself. Tears form in my eyes as I'm now in front of the man.

"Please!" I yell this time. My voice on the edge of hysteria.

My hand is raised toward the man's chest.

The man shakes his head in front of me and I memorize his blue eyes. He looks up at me, a faint smile forming on his lips.

"I know it's not you."

Tears stream down my face. I so desperately try to get control of my hand. But I can't.

"I'm sorry."

And with that, I scream as the dagger finds its home in the man's heart. I watch as the life drains from his eyes.

Aurelia forces my hand to stay on the dagger so I can feel the mans hot, red blood deep into my skin.

She makes me pull the dagger out of his chest and that's when I feel in control again.

I drop the dagger and I stare down at my bloody hand as Ameria speaks.

"That was your second lesson human. You don't always have a choice in this world."

I still stare down at my hand in a daze.

"You'll get used to it."

I snap my head up at Ameria. Get used to it?

That's when I lose it. I grab the dagger off the ground and I charge at Ameria.

My body stops in midrun but not before I throw the dagger at Ameria and it ends up stuck in her throne, blood splattering on her and the throne.

She looks at the dagger shocked and I smile to myself.

I'm in control of my body again and before I stop myself I let my mouth talk.

"Mine as well be covered in blood if you want to go around and kill people. It suits you."

I can see Ameria fist her hands together. I score.

"You're gonna regret this." She then looks over at Aiwin. "Aiwin, get her out of my sight."

Aiwin nods and grabs me by the upper arm, dragging me out.

When we're out of sight, Aiwin turns me so I'm facing him.

"Are you crazy?"

I smile to myself, wiping the blood on my clothes.

"After everything I've done so far. Yeah, I think so."

"Ameria could kill you in an instant. Because of that little act, she's gonna make sure your third trial will have you begging for your life to end."

"And why do you care if I live or die? Ameria is set on making me beg for death. And if I lie, she's gonna make sure I'm haunted for the rest of my life. I'm not gonna win. I either leave this place with immortality and Ameria lets me into this world and I'm haunted for the rest of my life or I die here."

"You won't die."

Aiwin leads me down back to my cell and grabs my hand covered in blood. "This means something. Not that you killed that man but that you're a fighter. You're still here fighting for what you want. You can do this."

"Why are you even telling me this?"

Aiwin backs away. "We all have our secrets. And when you make it out of this, I'll tell you everything."

I open my mouth to say something but Aiwin leaves, leaving me alone in darkness once again.

CHAPTER 27. BONDS

Blood. That's what I was covered in from head to toe. Red, hot, sticky blood. It was all around me.

I feel something slimy touch my legs. Just the hair of a touch to make the hairs on the back of my neck rise.

I stand still, listening, feeling until I hear the call of my name. Over and over.

"Who's there?"

Suddenly a dagger is in my hand, and floating in the blood are dead bodies. And in front of me are the four lives I've taken.

I jump with a start as I sit up in my cell. My breathing is heavy, my skin is slick with sweat.

It was just a nightmare.

But then I look around at my cell. I woke up from one nightmare to be brought back into another one.

I hug my knees into my chest and I slowly rock myself.

I miss the daylight; the sun heating my skin, the feeling of grass and dirt under my toes.

Instead, I'm stuck in this cell, surrounded by darkness and concrete.

I get up from where I sit and make my way to the door. I give it a pull but just like all the other times, it doesn't even budge.

Right as I'm pulling again, the door opens and in comes Aiwin and Aurelia in hooded black cloaks.

"You," I say Aurelia, as Aiwin closes the door.

I charge at her ready to swing my fist when Aiwin grabs my arm holding me back.

"Let go of me!"

"Relax. She's not going to do anything." Aiwin's voice is almost melodic, coated and soothing.

My muscles relax, and I slightly sag in Aiwin's hold as Aurelia moves her hood down.

"What a surprise Aiwin, I didn't know you have a bond with the human."

I can feel Aiwin's body tense behind mine as I slightly turn in his hold to see him.

"Bond?"

A look of surprise forms on Aurelia's face.

"You haven't told her?"

Aiwin moves away from me and before I can say anything he cuts me off.

"It's not a priority right now."

Aurelia's face softens when she faces me. She steps forward towards me but I take a step back.

She seems to notice and stops her advancement before looking over at Aiwin and back to me.

"You're a lucky girl."

I scrunch my eyebrows together.

"Why are you both even here?"

They both seem to contain their composure again and the air seems to get tense.

Aiwin is the first to speak. "We're here to get you out."

I shake my head. What a sick joke. "Get out of my sight."

Aurelia raises an eyebrow. "Such bold words to a Fae and Witch. She's got quite the mouth."

I snarl and she laughs before shrugging.

"Makes my job easier if you don't want to come. But I'm sure Jason will be quite heartbroken."

My defences fall. "Jason? You've spoken to him?"

"Yes. He's why I'm here and I need you to come with me. Aiwin is going to get us out."

My breathing becomes heavy, my palms sweaty.

"I've been here for so long."

Aiwin gently touches my shoulder. "It's time to get you out of here."

Aiwin pulls out the dagger sheathed in his thigh and hands it to me.

The daggers handle is curved to fit in the palm of my hand perfectly. Inside the handle looks to be almost blue liquid swirling gently on the inside and when it touches my hand, it glows softly and swirls a little faster.

"If you're ever in danger, use it. It will protect you."

I study the dagger a little longer before thanking him.

Aurelia then moves towards me pulling out another black cloak and helping me into it.

"You've gotten skinnier and weaker." She mumbles under her breath.

I ignore the comment as she helps me into the cloak. No doubt since I've been living off of bread and water for who knows how long.

"I'm surprised you've made it this long."

"She's stronger then you think," Aiwin says as he makes his way to the door.

I move my attention back to Aurelia.

"Why are you helping me?"

Aurelia stops and looks me in the eyes. She has Ameria's eyes, her mother's eyes.

"Jason promised me something in return."

I snort. "And here I thought you were doing this out of the goodness of your heart."

Aurelia ignores me and lifts up my hood. "Keep this on at all times. It'll cover you."

I pull on the hood to make sure it's as far as it'll go before looking back at Aurelia. "What did he promise you?"

"Now that is none of your business."

Aiwin opens the cell door and peaks outside before looking back at us. "Ready to go?"

I look back at my cell. At how dark and lonely it's been and a shiver runs through me. I rub my arms and look back at Aiwin and Aurelia.

"I'm ready to get out of this hell hole."

Aiwin nods and I follow him while Aurelia follows me from behind.

"Stay close." Aiwin whispers. "Grip the back of my shirt so I know you're still there. Tap once if something is wrong."

I nod but realize he can't see me. "Okay," I whisper.

I follow Aiwin through the cell halls, keeping my head down.

We take turn after turn, sometimes we hear people speaking up ahead but we never got close.

My grip tightens on Aiwin's shirt when we pass two creatures in the hall. I can feel Aurelia get closer to me but luckily the creatures keep to their business.

"We're almost there." Aiwin whispers.

I stay silent, too afraid to say anything. So close to freedom.

"Aiwin?"

That voice. My whole body begins to shake and my grip becomes tighter.

Suddenly Aurelia comes beside me and grips my arm and continues to pull me alongside her whole Aiwin turns and stops in the hall to Ameria.

We keep walking until Ameria calls out to us. "Aurelia, who's your friend?"

My heart stops and I can feel Aurelia's grip tighten on me.

"It's no one," Aurelia says.

But Ameria laughs. "I know it's you, human."

JASON

"We don't have enough Warriors to attack. We don't even know how big and how powerful Ameria's forces are."

I'm in the packhouse with Thomas, Alec and Rose, trying to think of the best way to get more warriors. Once Aurelia comes back successfully with Elizabeth, we're going to war with Ameria to put an end to her rule. But we don't know how many warriors she has on her end and how skilled they are.

"We could move the age down to teens?" Alec asks.

"No," I growl out. "We are not putting children out to fight."

I clench my fists together. There has to be something we can do. Anything.

"Well, then we're out of options," Alec states as he runs his hands through his hair.

"No."

I turn to Rose, all of our attention on her now.

"We have an option, but you're not going to like it."

"Well, we're out of options," Thomas says.

Rose moves forward, clenching the edge of the table.

"Rhazien has been trying to contact me. He wants me to join his clan."

Most of our jaws drop at this shock. I'm the first to speak.

"Rhazien, clan leader Rhazien?"

Rose rolls her eyes. "Yes. And I'm getting anxious about it. I'm part of nothing, not this pack and not to you. I told you I'd do anything to find Elizabeth and this is it. I can make a deal with him. To settle this urge to join a clan, I can have him offer some Vampires to fight. It might not work but it's worth the try."

A look of defeat has formed on her face and I can see Thomas move closer to her slightly.

I clear my throat. "You know you won't be able to leave him once you join the clan."

Rose nods. "I know. But Elizabeth would do it for me."

For the first time, I can see how close Elizabeth and Rose are. What they'd do for one another. I look over at my brother Thomas, my Beta, Alec. They are supposed to die for me. But if it ever came down to it, I'd die for them.

CHAPTER 28. ESCAPE

ELIZABETH

I stand still, too afraid to move. I don't know what to do. Ameria knows it's me.

I look at Aurelia from the corner of my eye and she slowly turns to face her mother.

She looks over at me one more time before her eyes begin to glow.

"Run."

It takes me a second to register what she said until I see black magic swirl in her hands and fire at Ameria.

I take off ignoring the fact that I really don't know where I'm going.

"Get her!"

I hear Ameria scream after me.

My heart pounds, my legs ache already from not having much food or water. Keep going, keep going, keep going. Don't stop.

I come to a split in the hallway and stop.

I don't know which way to go. I run a hand through my messy hair.

The sound of pounding feet against the floor makes me realize how scared I am. I'm just a human, I can't run fast, I don't have fangs or claws, I can't make magic in the palms of my hands. If they catch me, I'm dead.

That's when I feel it. Almost like an instinct has taken over.

I look down the right hallway and I feel it's almost calling to me.

I go right and I run as fast as I can go.

The footsteps have begun to get louder behind me.

They're catching up.

I don't want to get caught again. I can't get caught. Not now, not when I this close.

I come to another split in the hallway but I get this feeling, this whisper to go right.

So I go right without hesitation.

I run, even when my lungs are burning I continue to run, when my legs feel like they're on fire, I run.

Not just for me but for Rose, my best friend.

For Jason, my mate, my destined lover.

For my mom, even though she can't remember me.

And for my pack, because I am their Queen.

So I run. I run harder than I've ever run before.

A set of metal doors appear in front of me and I use all my weight and momentum from running to push through.

But the door is locked and I end up banging into the door and falling down on my back. The fall takes the breath out of me and I groan in pain as I roll over onto my stomach. Just great.

I lay there for a few seconds to fill my lungs with air, to get my composer together. My legs feel like jello, my vision moves in and out of focus.

No, don't pass out. Don't pass out. I need to stay awake. I need to get out.

I sit up and shakily get to my feet when I hear a hissing behind me. I stop in my spot, my heart beating fast. I shut my eyes tight as I slowly turn and re-open them to see one of the lizard creatures.

Dammit.

I feel my hands at my side begin to shake as the lizard slowly makes its way towards. I slowly move back with my hands out like I'm trying to calm a wild animal.

"Someone's scared." The lizard hisses and that's when I remember the dagger Aiwin gave me.

"Don't come any closer."

The lizard laughs and I feel myself shrink away. I mentally scold myself for showing fear and I pull out the dagger.

"I said don't come any closer."

The lizards head cocks to the side as if studying the blade and smiling.

"I can hear your heart, human. It beats, providing your life but it's also so weak. So easy to kill."

I tighten my grip on the dagger fearing the sweat on my hands will make me drop it.

The lizard continues to move towards me slowly and all I can hear is the blood rushing to my ears and the beat of my own heart.

Suddenly, the lizard looks at me strangely. The dagger I'm holding begins to glow.

"Your eyes," the lizard states and that's when I charge forward towards him and he charges towards me.

The dagger glows even more and I feel as if more power is pumping through my veins. I feel more confident, braver.

I charge onward and without thinking, I use the rocky wall as a lifting for my foot and I lunge into the air taking the lizard by surprise. My dagger finds its home in the lizard's neck and I hold on for dear life despite the green liquid pouring out of the lizard all over my hands and arms.

The lizard spins, trying to get me off him, but I hold on and kick off him with my feet, taking the dagger with me.

I roll on the ground and quickly manage to get into a low crouch as the lizard sways on his feet.

Green liquid drips off my dagger and onto the floor.

Where did I get all these moves from?

The lizard then falls to the floor, dead as I stay crouched, taking in everything I just did.

How did I just do that?

The dagger glows as if in response and I look down to it.

"Aiwin," I mumble.

The glows even more as if in response and a small smile forms on my face. He said his power is mine when I hold this dagger. He must be helping me.

"Thank you."

Footsteps sound from behind me and I quickly get up, turning to see my next opponent.

I'm about to charge forward when the cloaked figure stops.

"Wait!"

I recognize that voice.

"Aurelia?"

She moves her hood down before signing.

"I didn't think you'd make it this far."

I sheath my dagger back on my hip as Aurelia moves closer to me grabbing my arm.

"We need to go."

"Where's Aiwin?"

"Improvising."

She waves her hand towards the door and it opens to the darkness outside.

Aurelia pulls me forward through the doors outside and the first thing I notice is the wind hit my skin. The cool air against my hot skin.

Aurelia doesn't stop and continues to drag me forward away from Ameria's mansion.

Suddenly, a blast of dark magic flies past us and Aurelia pushes me to the ground. I look behind us to see Ameria on the steps of her mansion with warriors and those lizard creatures behind her.

I look her dead in the eyes and she does not look happy. She thrusts her hands forward and a ball of dark magic comes straight for me.

I gasp and I jump out of the way shielding my face while Aurelia moves swiftly in front of me firing back in Ameria's direction.

That's all it takes for the warriors and Lizards to come charging towards us.

Aurelia grabs me, pulling me off the ground and we run again into the barren forest surrounding Ameria's mansion.

My head swims, my legs shake to hold me up as we continue to run. I'm tired, so tired and Aurelia seems to notice.

"Hold on, we're almost there."

I nod before looking over my shoulder at Ameria's people coming after us in the distance.

"We're gonna be crossing her border soon. Do not let go of me."

"Okay," I say breathlessly.

We continue to run and soon a strong sensation comes over me. My skin pricks, my mouth tastes of metal.

Aurelia whispers a spell as my vision begins to tunnel.

Soon the ground is replaced with grass and the night sky is replaced with blue skies. I collapse to the ground, feeling the grass under my fingers and I almost cry. I have to shield my eyes as the daylight is too bright for me.

"Are we safe?" I ask.

Aurelia looks around at the meadow we dropped in to before looking back at me. A faint smile forms on her face.

"Yes. Your friends know we're here. The should be here soon."

That's all it takes for me to let my walls fall, to let all the emotion I was feeling in that cell to fall. I cry.

Sobs wrack my whole body and I feel Aurelia place a hand on my shoulder silently.

I hug my knees into my chest as I let the tears fall. I don't try to stop them.

I'm free.

I don't know how long it had been until I heard my name being called.

I look up to see Jason, Rose, Thomas and Alec all running towards me along with countless warriors behind them.

"Liz!"

I stare at them, too shocked to believe they're running towards me right now. It's been so long since I've seen them.

"They stop a couple feet away when they get close and a look of horror forms on their faces. A loud growl comes from Jason.

Jason.

I stare at him. At those deep blue eyes.

My mate.

"Jason," my voice is quiet and he kneels down and holds me in his arms.

"Liz?"

I look up to see Rose staring down at me and Jason moves so Rose can hug me. In the background, I can hear Aurelia speaking to Alec and Thomas.

"What happened to her?" Jason asks, turning to face Aurelia.

"Ameria barely fed her. She was stuck in a dark cell the whole time."

A loud growl comes from his chest and Jason kneels down next to me.

"I'm going to kill her."

"Step in line," Rose speaks up.

A few seconds later, that's when I feel the small pain in the back of my head, but I ignore it.

"You're here, you're really here."

Jason kisses my forehead, my cheeks and then my lips. His hands rub my arms and he gently cups my face before bringing his lips to mine.

"I missed you so much."

I bring my arms around Jason as he nuzzles his head in the crook of my neck.

"I missed you too."

I kiss his cheek and as I pull away, that's when the headache becomes even more painful and I groan.

I rest my head against Jason's chest as he lifts my chin up, looking down at me worriedly.

"You're hurting. What's wrong?"

"I—" My breathing becomes heavy and so does my head.

"Whoa, whoa, Elizabeth!"

I fall limp in his arms but I still manage to stay conscious.

"What's wrong?"

The world spins around me.

"Ameria barely fed her. She's weak. This could all be overwhelming for her. She hasn't seen daylight in forever." Aurelia says.

Jason tightens his hold on me as my head rolls back.

"We need to see the pack doctor. Now."

I feel Jason lift me up, a hand behind my back and knees.

My sight moves in and out of focus and so does what I hear.

"Liz, stay awake."

But I'm so tired. So much pain, so much energy has been

drained away from me.

"Liz—"

CHAPTER 29. BLOOD IS BLOOD

JASON

Elizabeth fell limp in my arms as I ran to the packhouse. Alec and Thomas both flanked me and Rose ran ahead of me, leading the way.

Multiple of my warriors were running around us to keep us safe.

Rose slows down to run beside me. "Give her to me. I can run faster."

I can't help it but growl. Our mate needs us.

"Jason, give her to me. I can get her there faster."

I look down at Liz before curing to myself.

I hand her off to Rose and before I know it she takes off.

I use the opportunity to shift into my wolf form to run even faster but Rose was right, she is the fastest here.

"She'll be okay." Alec mind links me. "She's strong."

I run harder. "I hope. She's only human. They're fragile."

Thomas speaks up into the link. "Elizabeth is stronger than most. She's still alive after Ameria took her. She'll make it through this."

My wolf pushes us even faster. We need to get to her.

The forest pasts by me in a blur. I don't even know if Aurelia was with us or not but I didn't care.

I see the packhouse in the distance and I run harder.

"Alpha," The pack doctor mind links me. "Rose has arrived at the packhouse. I'm dealing with the Luna right now."

I don't even respond as we reach the front steps of the pack house. We all shift and on the front steps are shorts for all my men. We change quickly and Alec, Thomas and I all make our way into the pack house.

I make my way into the living room to see Rose in the living room with her head in her hands. I scan the room to not see the doctor or Liz.

A growl emits from my chest and I move towards her grabbing onto her shoulders forcing her to look up at me with teary eyes.

"Where is she?"

She doesn't even say anything but her eyes dart to the left hallway.

I let go of her, making my way in that direction while I spot Thomas sit beside Rose on the couch.

Alec follows me from behind as I make my way down the hall and into the first room I see.

Elizabeth lays there unconscious on a table. The doctor looks up at me and moves toward me.

"I'm going to start an IV, she's very malnourished. Ameria barely gave her any food or water. Second, physically, besides cuts and bruises, everything is fine. Mentally, I think that's where she's gonna struggle."

I raise an eyebrow and move my attention to Elizabeth.

"She was trapped in a dark cell for a month apparently. Goddess knows what she was forced to do and what she went through. Thirdly, you two were separated for too long, the bond was weakened. It's a lot for her to take in."

I take in a deep breath. "Do you know when she'll wake up?"

"No, Alpha."

I clench my fists together and close my eyes to calm my temper.

"Do what you need to do."

I move to Elizabeth's side, sweeping her head to the side. "You're going to be okay."

I kiss her forehead before looking back at Alec.

"Where's Aurelia?"

ROSALYN

I sit on the couch with my head in my hands. I can feel Thomas rub my back soothingly as I feel tears slip down my cheeks.

What did Ameria do to Liz?

When I first saw her on the ground, that look in her eyes that I saw, empty.

I shake my head and I stand up. We need to fight back against Ameria.

"Rose?"

I turn back at Thomas standing there is in his black guardian uniform.

"Are you okay?"

I look away from him and I make my way to the door.

"I have business I need to take care of."

It took a while but I managed to contact Rhazian, the Vampire clan leader.

For a while, he's been trying to get me to join his clan knowing that I've been wanting to be part of something and not some lone Vampire. But I always refused. I never wanted to go with him. To leave Liz and this whole thing that has been going on. But things have changed now and because of what happened to Liz, what Ameria did to her, we'll need the extra help in fighting her back.

I currently walk through the forest at night. He told me he would find me here, where ever he is.

The night is quiet, but the air is humid and I know it's about to rain.

"Rose, so nice to see you."

I turn around to see Rhazian crouched on a tree branch with his black clothes and red cloak. I notice in the tree beside him is a younger male Vampire, wearing the same thing but a black cloak instead.

The jump off the trees and I can get a better look at the boy.

He has blonde hair swept to the side nicely. What should have been blue eyes I'd imagine are now red. His skin is pale, just like any other vampire but it seems to suit him. All in all, his strong jawline, eyes and hair make him an attractive person.

I turn my attention back to Rhazian who watches me intently.

"Have you reconsidered your decision on joining my clan?"

"Yes, but I want to make a deal."

Rhazian smiles, revealing his white, sharp teeth.

"A deal?"

I feel a drop of water hit me to know that it's about to rain.

"Yes, a deal."

"And what is this deal?"

I watch as the boy leans against a tree, arms crossed, listening.

"Ameria has started a fight with the Wolf Colony. She took the Luna and held her captive. We were able to retrieve her but we know Ameria is planning on attacking back and we know no one is happy with her ruling. I ask for you to give some of your Warriors to help us fight against Ameria and to take her down. In return, I will go with you."

The rain has now hit, down pouring on all of us but we don't care.

"So you want me to give some of my best warriors to fight alongside the wolves, one of our enemies and to take down Ameria for in return, a petty Vampire who has nowhere to go?"

I open my mouth to say something but Rhazian cuts me off.

"Do you think I am that desperate for you?"

"No, I—"

"You have nothing to offer besides yourself. I only want you so the wolves won't learn from you and possibly find weak points to possibly attack us in the future."

I stand there confused. That's why he wanted me.

Rhazian laughs. "Did you really think you were special? Besides that, I couldn't care less. Ameria may be a bad ruler, but anyone smart would know not to mess with her. She hasn't done anything that bothers me, therefore, I won't get into business that does not involve me."

"Please." My voice is weak, desperate as I remember Liz.

I look over at the boy who's blond hair now falls in front of his face because of the rain. He looks down at the ground looking like he's not even paying attention.

Rain drops down my own face covering the tears forming in my eyes.

"We need your help." My voice cracks.

Rhazian laughs.

"I don't care. Tell your wolf friends you're on your own."

"No—"

But before I know it, they're gone, running off.

I fall to my knees, mud splashing up onto me. I can't even help Liz when she needs me most. I let the rain pour down on me. I can't feel how cold it is so it doesn't matter.

In fact, I don't feel much anymore. I don't feel warmth, I'm not even alive.

I couldn't do anything as a human, I can't even do anything as a Vampire.

I'm useless.

CHAPTER 30. WHO WE ARE

JASON

"Explain everything to me."

Aurelia clicks her nails against the coffee table thinking to herself.

"What, no thank you?"

I growl and I shut my eyes to keep my wolf at bay. "You shouldn't test me right now."

Aurelia reveals a satisfied smirk and stands up, moving to the window.

"I can do what I want. You need me right now, you can't afford to lose me. I have the information you want. No one else saw what I saw."

I clench my fists, feeling my temper begin to take over and I clench my jaw knowing she's enjoying this. "Elizabeth saw. She was her prisoner."

Aurelia hums to herself and moves her hand down the drapes at the side of the windows. "That is true. But you don't know when she'll wake up. And by then it would be too late."

She moves swiftly across the room behind me, her nails trailing down my shoulder and arm before I snatch her wrist bending it back.

My wolf is ready to come out, he wants to rip her head off but she has information we need.

"Tell me."

Aurelia clicks her tongue and she bursts into darkness before reappearing at my side and sitting gracefully down on the couch.

"You're no fun anymore, Jason."

"Alpha, Jason." I correct.

Aurelia rolls her eyes. "Apologizes. So sorry if I offended you."

I growl again. "Get on with it."

Aurelia sighs. "Ameria took her to her mansion. It's warded off by magic: Enchanters, to be exact. It's an ancient spell even I've never heard of and that's why you couldn't locate her or feel her through the bond. It cuts off any communication. Now, Elizabeth was kept in her lowest floor, the cells. Down there are where most of her Warriors are. "Aurelia twirls her hand in the air and a hologram of dark magic appears, giving me the blueprints of the mansion.

"Elizabeth was kept here," a dot glows in one of the celled rooms. "She was guarded by one of Ameria's Shadows, a Fae warrior."

The ears perk up at this. "Aiwin?"

Aurelia's smile grows. "Precisely."

The Shadows, the best of the best warriors ever made. Fae born creatures who learn to fight at a young age. If you're ever in a battle with them, you're already dead.

I shake my head. "I thought he died."

"Oh, he's very alive. He was the one to guard her."

I run my hand through my hair. If Ameria has multiple Shadows, defeating her is going to be tough.

"Did you see Ameria?"

"No. I went in, retrieved Elizabeth, just like you said and got out."

I stare at Aurelia and I watch as she plays with her nails. She looks believable, but I did not miss the beat of her heart pick up.

I rush over to her, gripping her by her neck and lifting her up. I turn her head to the side, growling in her ear. "Liar."

Aurelia claws at my fist.

"You seem to forget that I can hear your heart. I know when you lie."

I let go and she drops to the floor coughing. I turn away back to my desk grabbing a pen and paper and throwing it at her hands.

"Now, let's start again, shall we? I want you to write down everything you know."

Aurelia stands with a grim expression. "I don't have to tell you anything."

"Not if you want the deal to fall through."

Aurelia picks up the pen and paper angrily, waves a hand at it and suddenly it's filled with writing, with everything she knows.

I snatch it away from her, examining it before she speaks.

"I'll have my best warriors here by tomorrow. You better keep your word, Dog."

I don't respond as she leaves, disappearing into thin air.

I sigh, running my hand through my hair before taking the paper and sitting in a seat.

I read it all over multiple times and I get angrier each time.

My mate was put through hell. I close my eyes and even out my breathing to try and calm myself before a knock comes at my door.

"Yes?"

The door opens and Alec and Thomas both walk in.

"What is it?"

Alec is the first to speak.

"Rose went to speak with Rhazian."

I move my papers aside, standing up at the news.

"And?"

This time Thomas speaks up. "She was unsuccessful."

I bring my fist down on the table. "Dammit!"

That was our last hope to get more warriors to fight against Ameria. Our chances now are slim. We don't know her army or how powerful they are.

"We need more warriors."

Alec steps forward, placing down Rogue documents. "I have an idea."

I pick up the papers, examining them. These are the rogue prisoners I hold.

I look up at him, raising an eyebrow.

"What if we were to take out our prisoners. They're rogues, all they want to do is fight. Others just want to leave. Why don't we give them an opportunity."

I sit back down, thinking this through. "Opportunity?"

"Well more of a bargain. They help fight against Ameria and after they are free. No longer prisoners."

I shake my head. "Alec, as desperate as we are, we are not that desperate. That's letting a bunch of criminals and dangerous wolves roam my colony. My people could get hurt and I will not allow that. Lives are already going to be lost because of Ameria. I don't want to have to deal with more killings after."

Alec's shoulder slump in defeat. "We need more options here. We need bend the rules a little."

"Letting rogues out is more than bending, Alec."

Thomas shifts on his feet. "We have to do something here. What other options do we have?"

"I don't know. But for now, continue to train our warriors."

Thomas and Alec both nod, leaving the room.

As the door closes I grab the nearest thing near me, a glass of water and I throw it across the room at the wall before sitting back down, my head in my hands.

I don't know what to do. For the first time, I'm lost. Ameria will win if we can't get more warriors. I can't do anything. I need help. I need Elizabeth.

CHAPTER 31. FOR YOU

ROSALYN

Training had become a part of my life now. Every morning I'd change and run over to where all the werewolves trained and I'd learn alongside them to help fight against Ameria.

However, even though I was on the Werewolves side, they still gave me that look that they didn't want me here, to leave because I was an enemy, not a friend.

Despite this though, I still came. Every day I'd come and train. Not for them or Jason or even Ameria. But for Elizabeth, who still lies motionless in a bed.

I shake the thought out of my head. She'll be fine.

I put my hair up into a ponytail and run laps with everyone else to begin warmup.

If I can't get Rhazian to join the fight against Ameria, the least I can do is fight alongside Jason's Colony.

As I'm running I catch a figure in the distance along the tree line. I squint my eyes and I notice who it is, the boy who came with Rhazian when I came to speak with him.

He still wears the same black cloak, his hair appears more golden in the sunlight. His skin must have been sun-kissed before he became a Vampire.

From the distance that he is at, I can still hear him speak to me with my enhanced hearing.

"We need to talk."

I look around nervously to see if anyone sees what I'm seeing.

No one will even notice me slip off anyway. No one pays attention to the Vampire.

I use my speed and I run off in the blink of an eye before anyone.

Before I know it, I'm standing in front of the boy.

"What do you want?"

The boy smirks, playful even. "Wow, straight to the point. How about a, hello? Maybe, nice to see you?"

I scoff. "Nice to see you my ass."

"Follow me."

I hesitate as he disappears into the forest but really at this point, I got nothing to lose.

I follow after him, moving branches out of the way.

"Why did you come here?"

The boy keeps moving forward, walking silently.

"And who are you?"

The boy suddenly stops and turns to look at me. An amused smile spreads across his face revealing straight, white teeth. "I'm Kane. Rhazian's second in command."

Kane bows down in front of me I'm a cocky manner.

"Pleasure to meet you, Rosalyn."

I take a step back, snarling, going into defensive mode. If Rhazian's second in command is here for me, something is up. "What do you want?"

"Rhazian doesn't know what's best. He doesn't know when to take an opportunity, so I'm here to help."

I raise an eyebrow. "Help? What do you want in return? I know you wouldn't offer to help for free."

Kane looks up at the sky. "True. But what could I possibly want? I live forever, I can get anything I desire."

"You tell me."

"I want to overthrow Rhazian. I'll give you my best and in return, you'll help me and become part of my Clan."

If I was able to breathe, I'm sure my breath would have caught.

"You want to be a leader? What's wrong with Rhazian?"

"He's old, tired. He never wants to get involved. Us Vampires, we like to have fun. We're bored."

"Bored? So will the same happen to you once they get bored?"

Kane smiles excitingly. "Oh love, they'd never get bored of me."

I scoff but still think over this offer. Jason is desperate for help and here is Kane, offering it. If I turn this offer away, I might not be able to forgive myself if Ameria destroys us.

"That's it then? That's the deal?"

Kane tilts his head. "You make it seem like it's nothing. But yes, that is the deal."

I lick my lips nervously, clench and unclench my hands. What else do I have to lose?

"How many are you offering?"

"One hundred."

My eyebrows raise. "Rhazian won't notice one hundred warriors gone?"

Now Kane scoffs. "Rhazian hardly notices anything."

I look at Kane. Would it be worth it? Get the help we need against Ameria, win against her. Would Kane be better for the Vampire Colony? Perhaps not, but he's nowhere close to the threat Ameria brings. We could always deal with him later. I could deal with him later since I would be part of the clan.
"Fine. You have a deal."

Kane's smile grows and he pulls out a knife. He brings it to his palm, slicing the skin, black blood seeping through.

"Seal in blood."

So I grab my own knife, cut myself on the hand and watch as my own blood seeps through the cut.

We both bring our hands together, completing the deal. Both our cuts heal almost immediately after.

"Pleasure doing business with you, Rosalyn."

I stay silent as Kane runs off deeper into the forest.

What have I just done?

JASON

I feel myself being shaken, my name being heard over and over again. I awake startled, Alec before me waking me up.

I look around me, seeing I'm in my office, sitting at my desk. I must have fallen asleep while working.

I rub my eyes and I look up at Alec. "Sorry, Alec. What's wrong?"

"Rosalyn would like to speak with you. She said it's important."

I rub my eyes once more to get rid of the grogginess. I've been working basically twenty-four seven. No breaks.

I nod and a second later Rosalyn comes into the room.

"What's wrong Rose?"

"I got us more warriors. One hundred extra."

This has me sitting straighter in my seat. "You got one hundred extra warriors? Where did these numbers come from?"

"Kane. Second on command of Rhazian, Vampire Colony."

I scrunch my eyebrows together. "I thought they weren't going to assist."

"Well let's just say he had a change of heart."

I look over at Alec who looks just as surprised as me.

"What was the cost?"

"Don't worry, I dealt with it."

Rose turns to leave but Alec moves in front of her.

"Rose, what was the cost?"

She stays silent and a growl erupts from my chest.

"Don't make me ask again."

Rose turns, looking sad. "I did what I had to. For you and Elizabeth. You'll find out soon enough."

And with that she takes off, leaving me and Alec with this news. I might be able to protect the Colony and Elizabeth now but nothing comes from free. Whatever Rose agreed to, I know was not easy.

Suddenly, Thomas rushes into the room, excitement in his eyes.

"Jason, Elizabeth is awake."

CHAPTER 32. AWAKEN

ELIZABETH

Darkness was all that I saw. I heard nothing—well, sometimes I would hear my name like people were talking to me. But for days, maybe even months it had been like this. Time wasn't of the essence, I didn't mind being alone here but in fact, it was peaceful considering everything that had happened to me.

 liked peaceful, I want to stay here. But slowly, the darkness begins to fade. Black turning to grey and I knew what was happening.

No, I don't want to go back. Not to that world.

I desperately urged the darkness to stay. I begged. But no matter how hard I tried, the darkness began to fade, I felt something tug at me, pulling at me but I didn't go easy.

No, I wasn't going to go easy.

The grey around me began to turn to a soft fluffy white. It was even a tad comforting.

People I knew began to flash across my vision: Jason, Rose, Alec, Thomas, mom. All these people I love and I suddenly felt this pain in my chest. Heartache maybe?

Suddenly the white began to lift and before I knew it, my eyes were fluttering open to the insistently lit room.

"Liz?"

My eyes flutter open and I turn to see Rose holding my hand in hers.

Her eyes are wide and for the first time, I feel how cold her hand is.

"You're awake."

I slowly sit up taking in where I am.

"I made it back."

Rose let's out a small laugh. "Yeah, you did."

The door to the room suddenly opens and Jason, Alec, and Thomas all rush in.

Jason stops and stares at me for about a whole solid minute

before rushing to my other side and crushing his lips to mine.

I realize how much I miss this—his warmth, his touch. I realize how much I miss the sparks, the tingles that seem to dance on my skin when he touches me.

It's almost overwhelming.

Jason rests his forehead on mine. "You're finally awake. You're here."

I nod, almost not believing it myself. "I'm here."

Jason's eyes cloud over momentarily. "I just mind-linked the doctor."

"I'm fine."

"No, you're not." Rose cuts in.

She stares at me with a blank expression, devoid of any emotion.

She almost speaks in a whisper. "Have you seen yourself?"

Her voice takes me off guard.

I turn to look at Jason, Alec and Thomas, all of whom turn their gaze to the floor silently. Only Rose keeps her gaze.

"Your skin," Rose grabs for my hand. "Is as pale as mine. Your eyes, were pure gold: Jason's eyes from when he bit you. His power in his veins was the only thing keeping you alive. You lost weight. And when I looked at you, when I looked at my best friend who was kneeling on the ground, a part of you just seemed, gone."

My breathing picks up and I look away down at my hands.

Fingers lift my chin up gently and I look up to see Jason looking at me worriedly.

"What happened to you?"

Images flash across my vision: my cell, the people I killed, Ameria.

I break eye contact with Jason and move out of his grip feeling tears sting my eyes.

It was real, all of it. The people I killed, my blood stained hands.

I run a hand through my hair, my breathing picking up.

"Liz?"

I look back at Jason, my vision blurry from the buildup of tears.

"I—I killed all those people."

Jason wraps his arms around me.

"I did it. I killed them."

Jason rubs my back soothingly as I hear the door to the room open and shut.

"You're okay."

I push away holding my head in my hands. "No, no it's not okay."

"Elizabeth," Jason answers weakly.

I lift my head up to meet his gaze feeling anger push through. "Are you not listening to me? I killed them! I killed innocent people! How is that okay?"

"Liz, your eyes—"

"I don't care about my eyes!"

"They're glowing."

I sit back, rubbing my eyes. "Yeah, they do that now."

Jason opens his mouth to say something but the door opens and the doctor walks through.

"Alpha."

The doctor bows his head in respect as he moves towards me.

The moment he lays a hand on me, I flinch involuntarily and Jason growls at the doctors.

"Sorry, my fault." I look over at Jason who eyes the doctor and I place my hand on Jason's.

"It's okay."

He moves his attention to me, his black eyes returning to his natural colour, his wolf backing off.

I smile softly at him before turning to the doctor and my eyes widen.

I feel my blood drop, my heartbeat pick up.

He looks exactly like the one man I killed back at Ameria's mansion.

His face is bloody and he stares right back at me.

I can hear a murmur in the background, I feel my body being shaken and suddenly, the bloody-faced man reaches out to me and darts across the bed to stand on the other side of the bed.

I move my hand down to my thigh to grab the dagger Aiwin gave me, but it's no longer there. Panic gnaws at my chest and I look around the room for a weapon.

I look up and the man moves towards me as I feel hands on my arms, turning me around.

I panic, hitting a figure behind only to face Jason and I feel myself calm down.

His hands find my shoulders and he embraces me as the world around me returns.

"Liz, what's wrong?"

I move out of his embrace, turning to face the doctor whose face has returned. I can feel my panic disintegrate and I turn back to face Jason.

"I—I thought I saw-" I stop speaking. What am I going to say? That I'm seeing things? Having flashback memories. They're going to think I'm crazy.

"Nothing. Probably just a panic attack or something."

Jason's eyes narrow for a second and his eyes dart to the doctor then back to me before embracing me again before the doctor begins running me through some tests.

I'm okay. What I saw wasn't real.

I'm okay.

CHAPTER 33. PANIC

Today is the first time I'm going outside. Jason is beside me, almost never leaving my side since I've been rescued.

For some reason, I feel as if there's this barrier between us. Almost as if time away has diminished our bond. The doctor said that I was so weak upon arrival because the bond was snapping back into place after my absence. But after a week, it still isn't the same.

Maybe it's me and what I've been through or maybe it's the war brewing with Ameria, but things have changed.

"Are you okay?" Jason speaking snaps me out of my thoughts.

"I'm fine."

We enter the weapons room where all the bows and arrows sit. I observe the wall with a dull daze.

"We can do this another day if you're not ready."

Jason puts a comforting hand on my arm but I shrug him away maybe a bit too forcefully.

"No, I can do this." I breathe out.

I haven't touched a weapon or any of my bows since what Ameria made me do. How she forced me to kill innocents with something I loved to do—archery.

I take a black bow in my hands and I let my fingers follow the smooth curve of the bow.

How I used to hold this before.

Ringing sounds in my ears and I look up to see the wall that used to be covered with beautiful bows, are now covered in red blood.

I drop the bow I'm holding in shock and Jason puts a hand on my shoulder.

"What's wrong?"

I look at Jason's worried eyes and when I look back at the wall, it's just the bows again.

"Elizabeth?"

I silently pick up the bow and I place it back on the wall, silently walking away.

I sit on the edge of my bed alone. What is even happening to me? It's like the life has been sucked out of me.

Even though I was rescued, Ameria did somewhat win. She took away a part of who I was.

My heart rate begins to pick up and my breathing intensifies. My palms become clammy and I begin to have a hard time getting air to my lungs.

I shut my eyes as I try to get rid of the panic attack taking over when suddenly I open my eyes and I look over at the nightstand where sits the dagger Aiwin gave me.

Everyone questioned what it was and I simply said I picked it up during the escape.

I haven't touched it since I got here and I wasn't going to bother. But as I stare at it, it seems to slightly glow warmly to me.

I stare at it more closely and the blade seems to glow brighter.

I slowly bring my hand towards it, cautiously.

When my hand lands on the hilt, it feels warm to the touch and I feel a calming effect come over me.

"Aiwin," I whisper and the blade glows warmly at me as if being called.

I smile to myself and I grip the dagger, holding it for the first time I got here.

I open my mouth to say something when my door suddenly opens and I tuck the dagger quickly behind me and into the waistline of my pants.

Rose steps into the room, her brows furrowing together when she sees me.

"Everything okay?"

I nod.

"Well, I thought you'd like to know that Jason is holding a meeting to discuss the attacks against Ameria."

I swallow heavily. "Already?"

"Jason got the numbers he needed. He's ready to fight back."

I look down at the ground. This is happening fast. How could he have gotten the numbers this fast?

"You should be ready to."

I look up at Rose.

"It's time we bring Ameria down for everything she's done. She's hurt too many."

I can feel the dagger warm against my skin soothingly, almost as if its . . . comforting me.

"How could Jason have gotten the numbers to fight against Ameria already?"

Rose avoids my eye contact. "We've all had to sacrifice something."

I raise an eyebrow, my curiosity growing. "Sacrifice what?"

I can see Rose clench her hands before facing me. "Here, come on. Jason will explain everything. As Queen of this colony, you need to hear this."

I almost stop dead in my tracks. Queen. I haven't heard that word in a while.

"Rose, it's been a while since I fulfilled my role as a Luna, Queen, even as a mate to Jason. Do you think—"

"Yes, you can do this. You survived Ameria's clutches and you're ready to fight back for what you want."

I look down at the ground mumbling, "What I want."

Rose tilts her head to the side with a curious look. "What do you want, Liz?"

I shake my head, feeling the dagger warm my side. "I don't know," I whisper. "I don't know what I want anymore."

For the first time in who knows how long, I'm entering a meeting with all the Alphas in the colony.

A long table fills the room where the Alphas sit around it. A little off is almost what you would call a throne where Jason sits, listening to the Alphas inputs.

The room quiets when I enter and all eyes land on me as I

make my way to stand beside Jason's throne.

"Liz, we're just discussing when we should make the first attacks."

"Already?"

Jason nods before turning his attention back to the Alphas. "We have the numbers now."

The discussion begins but I interrupt. "Where did these numbers come from? Couldn't have just pulled them out of your ass with no price."

Jason raises an eyebrow.

"How did you get the numbers?"

Jason looks at the Alphas and then me. "Witches and Vampires. We're working together."

I stand there looking back and forth between the Alphas sitting and Jason.

"How? You hate Vampires and Witches don't get along with anyone."

At that moment, the door to the room opens and Aurelia walks in, the click of her heels the only noise.

"I wouldn't say that's the truth."

I take a step back, moving my hand behind me to grab my dagger. "What is she still doing here?"

Jason sees the small action and stands, putting a hand on my shoulder.

"No, she's an ally."

"What?"

The Alphas stir uncomfortably as Aurelia takes a seat.

"And here I thought we'd become friends after I saved your precious mate."

I can see Jason clench his jaw before I turn my attention to Aurelia.

"Why did you save me?"

Aurelia leans back and crosses her legs before smiling at me.

"I don't believe that is what we're here to discuss."

I take a step forward before Jason grabs my arm.

"She's right. We're here to discuss a war. Aurelia is

154

representing the Witches at this table."

I scan the table before turning to Jason.

"And the Vampires?"

"Me."

Suddenly, a blonde male leans against the wall and in the blink of an eye, he's in front of me reaching for my hand.

"Kane. It's a pleasure to meet you."

His cold lips touch my hand and I take my hand a bit too forcefully but Kane just smiles before sitting at the table.

"Why are you all helping us?"

Aurelia and Kane look up at me, their expressions matching: satisfaction.

Kane is the one to speak. "Everything has a cost. Did you really think we'd do this out of good will?"

I stay silent before I turn to Jason. "What was the price?"

Jason swallows. "We were desperate. We needed numbers. So, Aurelia made a deal with me to save you from Ameria and to give us her best fighters. In return, she would rule after Ameria'a downfall."

My eyes nearly jump out of my sockets. "You what?"

Aurelia laughs behind me.

"You gave Aurelia—Ameria's daughter, the woman we're trying to take down— power over the colonies? Are you crazy?"

"She saved you."

"I'm one person. Not a world."

I can see anger flash behind Jason's eyes but I turn away from him to Kane.

"What did you get for your generosity," I spit.

Kane smiles at me. "Rosalyn. But it shouldn't matter, she's only one person. Not a world."

CHAPTER 34. FIGHT

I never left a place so fast after what Kane told me.

I could hear Jason calling after me but I ignored him as I made the flight of stairs, down the hall and into Rosalyn's room. I let the door slam shut behind me only to hear it open again, Jason letting himself in.

"Liz,"

"Shut up."

Rose sits in her bed, drinking a red beverage, no doubt blood.

She looks up at me and narrows her eyes before putting her drink down.

"What's wrong?"

"Why didn't you tell me?"

Her eyes turn to Jason's before returning to mine.

"Because I knew this would happen."

I move to sit beside her but she stands and makes her way to me.

"We needed more men and this was our last option."

"He's going to take you away. Away from me."

Rose smiles faintly before turning away. "Liz, ever since we've come here all there's been is pain. We've both already suffered. I died, Liz. Ameria, she broke you. You can't even hold up a bow without having a panic attack."

I look over at Jason who looks at me with sad eyes and puts a hand on my arm before nodding. I look down at the ground, swallowing hard.

"We'll work through it like we always do."

Rose turns around with an intense look in her eyes. "Liz, I don't want us to be in pain. With Ameria ruling, she will always be after us, you, Jason, our families." Rose shakes her head, her voice faltering. "No, no I won't have this. Kane can help and if this is the price we have to pay then so be it."

Jason's hand travels down to my hand and squeezes it slightly. "Liz, you know this is what has to be done."

I turn to him, feeling tears build up in my eyes.

"I'll never see you again, Rose."

Suddenly within the blink of an eye, Rose is embracing me.

"But it'll be worth it. We will find some sort of peace."

I shake my head. "That's a lie."

Rose pulls back and shrugs. "Maybe, maybe not. But we have to try. This is the only way."

"Rose—"

Roses eyes suddenly glow a red angrily. "You don't tell me what to do. Stop trying to be the hero, the one who makes all the right decisions." Rose's voice is sharp, almost like a blade. The way she looks at me makes me feel like I'm getting stabbed with every word.

Rose prowls towards me, her expression angry.

Jason growls as Rose gets closer to me, his own eyes glowing and his claws begin to extend. Rose snarls at him through her fangs and he returns a growl.

"Enough!" I yell.

I turn my attention back to Rose who stares at me like a predator just found its prey.

She shakes her head. "You're not the hero. You let me die and here I am trying to help you, you're mate, your colony!"

Rose is at the other side of the room in a split second and punched a mirror, it shattering beneath her fist.

"Rose . . ."

Rose tilts her head up towards Jason. "We've all sacrificed something for you, your turn."

Rose charges towards Jason with her super speed and collides with him. Her speed knocks them both back, crashing through a window two stories down.

"Jason!"

I feel my chest squeeze, feeling a full effect of the mate bond pull as I feel his pain.

I run up to the window looking down to see Jason shift in time. Rose stands a few feet away, fangs extended.

I hear the door open and Alec and Thomas rush into where I stand. "Luna, are you okay?"

"Yes, I'm fine, but they're not!" I point down towards where

Rose and Jason are currently fighting and both Alec's and Thomas's eyes fade as they all communicate with one another.

Alec turns to Thomas suddenly. "Stay with her." He jumps out the window, shifting midway through before Thomas grabs my arm, pulling me away.

"No." I pull my arm away but his grasp is too strong.

Stupid werewolf genes.

Thomas begins dragging me away from the window, my view of Rose, Jason, and Alec disappearing.

"Thomas, let me go."

I pull my arm harder and he begins to squeeze my arm harder.

"Thomas you're hurting me."

His eyes widen and he lets go. "I'm sorry."

I use the opportunity of freedom to run to the window and I climb outside, holding onto the brick to climb down.

"Luna!"

Thomas stares at me with worry as I climb down.

The sounds of snarls and growls fill the air as I make my descent.

I hear the sound of clothes ripping and I look up to see Thomas shifting into his wolf.

He leaps from the window, waiting for me at the bottom.

I land on the ground and come face to face with Thomas's Wolf.

I look behind him to see Rose get slashed by Jason.

Blood drips from her chest but she ignores it and jumps onto him.

Alec stands there wanting to intervene, but if Jason has given him orders to stay then he must.

I move my attention back to Thomas's wolf.

"Move."

His wolf doesn't break eye contact with me and I feel my patience break.

I pull the dagger Aiwin gave me.

"I said move!" I bark.

Thomas's eyes widen and he bows his head slightly letting me pass.

I grip the dagger and I make my way to Jason and Rose. My vision suddenly becomes sharp, observant as I walk closer to them.

"Enough!"

But they continue to fight like they didn't even hear me.

I grip the dagger even harder and I make the decision to grab Rose's arm.

"I said enough!"

She looks at me, her red eyes glowing and Jason stops, looking at me.

I suddenly realize the dagger is glowing in my hand.

"Stop fighting, both of you."

Rose snarls.

"Enough of this." I put the dagger away.

"I'm sacrificing everything for this asshole!" I glare at Rose and she suddenly backs away, her head slightly down.

"Go take care of your injuries."

Rose gives me one last look before walking away.

I turn my attention to Jason who's still in his wolf form.

"Never tell Thomas to hold me back. Or I'll be the one fighting you next time."

With that, I walk off. How lovely it is to have everything falling apart.

CHAPTER 35. WAR
PART 1

It's amazing how life can change in a matter of seconds. Ever since I've been brought into this world, I've slowly watched all those I've loved fall apart and I haven't been able to do anything about it. I may be Queen of the wolves, mate to the King, but I still don't have the power to help those around me.

I sit on the edge of my bed listening to the quiet of the night. I haven't spoken to anyone, not since the fight with Jason and Rose. My bond with Jason is falling apart, I can feel it getting weaker and weaker and I don't know why. Something is happening.

I let out a breath. This war is breaking everything. It's breaking me, or whatever is left of me.

A knock sounds at the door and I jump slightly before the door opens and Jason leans against the door frame, arms crossed.

"Hey."

I turn my head the other way as I hear his footsteps come close and the bed sag beside me.

"What do you want Jason?"

I want to see my mate."

I snort before turning to him. "Since when have you really been treating me like your mate?"

Jason's eyebrows scrunch together. "What?"

"You've barely spoken to me. You don't touch me or kiss me or show me anything." I wrap my arms around me. "Rose was right. We've all sacrificed so much but what have you given up?"

Jason's hands clench together. "What are you talking about? I'm constantly out in the field training warriors to fight against Ameria, to protect you and my colony. Every day I'm sacrificing time. I could be with you now or I could be with you for as long as I would like afterwards."

"You have Alec to train the Wolves Aurelia for the Witches and Kane for the Vampires. It's not just you! I've been struggling every day since I've been rescued from Ameria's grasp."

I turn away from Jason and I study the night sky feeling my voice break. "There are moments when I can't breathe. When I feel alone and I'm suffocating. I feel like she's watching me or she's going to take me again. Jason growls. "She won't take you away from me again."

I feel arms wrap around me, his warmth surrounding me. I feel soft kisses against my cheek and own my neck and I place my hands on his arms. I close my eyes enjoying this moment of closeness, of him just touching me, feeling his breath against my skin.

I turn around to face him, planting a kiss on his lips before resting my head on his chest. He wraps his arms around me.

"You won't ever be taken away from me."

I look up into his eyes. The eyes I got so distracted from when I first met him and I kiss him deeply, wholeheartedly until I'm out of breath and when I catch my breath again I kiss him with just as much passion.

Jason suddenly pulls away, looking me deeply in the eyes. "I'm sorry."

"For what?"

"For not being a proper mate. For not calling you beautiful every day, for not asking how you are, if you're okay. I have been selfish, I haven't been observant over everyone and that's my job as a King. I've been so distracted at what Ameria can do that I don't want it to happen again."

Jason begins tracing the mark on me with his index finger letting my breath catch. "The bond is breaking because I haven't shown I love you, Liz." He leans in, kissing me gently on the lips before looking back into my eyes and aligning my hand with his. "I promise you Elizabeth that from here on out I will be a proper mate. I will show you I love you every day and I will make sure you are always safe and protected."

I lay there, staring into his eyes, shocked at his words, speechless. So I kiss him with everything I have and for the rest of the night, we lay there in each other's arms.

I woke up in Jason's arms in the morning and it was the best sleep I've had in a while. No nightmares.

I slowly lift his arm off my waist and swing legs to beds edge. I quietly make my way to the bathroom to turn the shower on.

I look at my appearance in the mirror only to be horrified at my wreck of hair.

"Dammit," I mutter.

Shaking my head, I strip down and step into the shower. When I'm done, I wrap a towel around me and I step back into the room to retrieve my clothes only to be met with a half-naked Jason.

He sits on the edge of the bed, eyes wide and staring at my chest and legs. His eyes darken and I move slowly to retrieve my clothes, my eyes never leaving him.

"Um, I'm just going to," I point to the bathroom and pick up my clothes. "Uh, yeah."

I quickly move to the washroom and I close the door with a silly smile on my face.

After changing, I open the door only to see Jason is gone. I decided to make my way to the kitchen to be met with Thomas who is leaning against the counter, drinking orange juice.

He bows his head slightly as I enter the kitchen and I shake my head at his formalities. "Luna, anything I can get for you?"

I open the fridge to pour myself a glass of orange juice as I stand across from Thomas. "Do you know where Jason went?"

Thomas's eyebrows raise slightly. "Oh, I think he got called to help with something in the colony."

"Oh," I say feeling disappointment take over.

Thomas seems to notice this and he puts down his glass. "Your archery could use some work."

Visions suddenly flash across my mind of what Ameria made me do and I have to put down my glass.

"You haven't done it in a while."

The faces of those I killed cross my mind and I close my eyes.

That won't ever happen again.

"Luna?"

I open my eyes and do my best to smile.

"Sounds like a good idea."

"Awesome." Thomas grabs the glasses in the sink before turning to me. "Let's head down there."

"Try again," Thomas says as the arrow flies past the target for the fifth time. "Your hands shake too much, steady your hands."

I glare at him before I lick my lips nervously. I grab another arrow and I pull back the string.

Focus. Look where you want to go. Easy.

Focus, focus, focus. My hands begin to shake, but I just ignore it. I try to even out my breathing, to calm myself and stop the shaking.

Focus. This is easy.

My whole arm begins to shake slightly.

This is not Ameria's mansion.

I am not killing, this is a target. I repeat the thought over and over.

I let the arrow fly and it catches the edge of the target.

I exhale, biting my cheek. "Dammit."

"Well, at least you hit the target this time."

"Shut up, Thomas."

He puts his hands up defensively as I aim again.

I breathe out, I pull the string back and . . .

Fail.

I stare at the stupid target. If Ameria's forces were to attack now I'd surely be dead.

"Maybe today is just not your day."

I laugh. "You counting all the days before this too?"

Thomas looks down at the ground and I shake my head.

"I'm done here."

"Luna—"

"No. Just—" I breathe in deeply and I close my eyes. "Just give me a moment."

My chest feels like it's squeezing, my heart rate beats faster.

"Are you okay?"

I look up to Thomas and he takes a step back.

"Your eyes . . ."

I shut my eyes. Jason's genes are coming to surface.

"I'm fine."

"Are you sure you're—"

The sound of screaming cuts him off and I open my eyes to see him looking at the area around us. More screams come from the distance in the village.

Thomas suddenly moves towards me, grabbing my wrist. "We need to go, now."

I quickly pick up my bow and I secure my quiver as he drags me along. We travel through the forest, up the hill to make it to the packhouse. But a scream so loud, so ear piercing draws my attention to my left and I yank my wrist out of Thomas's grip.

"No, Luna—"

He doesn't finish as I run to my left, letting the tree branches scratch me. But my wrist is grabbed again by a very annoyed and panicked Thomas.

"You can't go there. The village is in that direction."

"They obviously need help."

A scream answers and I unsuccessfully try yanking my wrist out of his grip.

"Let me go, Thomas."

"I have orders."

This time I look at Thomas, my anger rising. "I said, let me go. Now. I am your Luna and you *will* respect me."

Thomas bows his head slightly and lets go of my wrist.

"You are free to join me but don't ever take me somewhere against my will."

I continue to make my way in the directions the screams are coming from. I can hear Thomas not far behind me and as the screams get louder, I slow my pace and make my way behind a bush. I look over at Thomas only to see his eyes look slightly foggy and distant. He must be in a mind link right now.

I peak past the bush to see bodies on the ground, wolves snarling and snapping at that lizard like creatures that I saw at Ameria's mansion. That must mean . . . Ameria is here.

Buildings are set on fire, puddles of blood shower the ground. Multiple guard wolves attack the creatures, ripping them apart but there's so many of them.

A loud horn sounds off in the distance, over and over. An alarm.

A scream brings my attention back to the village. One of the creatures is making an advance onto a little boy.

Tears stream down his face and he hugs a teddy bear close to his chest.

I react on instinct by loading my bow and aiming.

"I can do this," I breathe.

I pull back the string, aiming at the creatures back. My hands begin to slightly shake, my breathing becomes uneven.

The boy screams louder and the creatures hand reaches out to the boy.

'Let it fly," Rose would always tell me. 'Take the shot, you can do this.' Just like that day at the tournament. I felt so distracted and I couldn't get my thoughts in order. I had trouble focusing.

Another scream brings my focus back to the scene in front of me and my hands stop shaking, my breathing becomes even and I let the arrow fly.

A grunt of pain comes from the creature, the arrow lodged into its back. This brings the attention of a wolf and it snarls, jumping onto the creature, burring its teeth into its neck, killing the creature.

Despite the danger of doing so, I run out of my hiding spot and towards the crying boy.

"Luna!"

I run past all the fighting only to be clotheslined by an arm, my back hitting the ground hard beneath me, the breath being knocked out of me.

A creature looms before me and as it moves its arm up to slash me, a wolf pounces the creature, taking it down beside me.

I roll onto my side to see the wolf rip out the creature's throat, blood dripping down its teeth and chin.

The wolf stares at me and I look into its eyes. I smile relieved.

"Thanks, Thomas."

I get up onto my feet, grabbing the boy. Thomas lowers himself and I reluctantly climb onto his back as he runs up the hill and towards the packhouse to safety.

CHAPTER 36: WAR

PART 2

Thomas runs fast making me hold onto his fur for support. All around us, Jason's wolves fight against Ameria's creatures, clearing a safe path for their Luna.

Thomas doesn't slow down and keeps running towards the packhouse. As we get closer, Ameria's creatures lessen as they haven't gotten that close yet.

Many warriors crowd the area at the Pack House and many are getting ready in waves to be sent out against Ameria's attack.

I scan the crowds of people and wolves, trying to make out any familiar faces. As Thomas stops, get off his back noticing a familiar figure not too far, instructing warriors what to do.

Alec.

I run towards him, relieved to see another familiar face.

"Alec!"

He spins, turning towards with the wide eyes full of relief.

"Thank the Moon Goddess you're alright." His eyes scan me, looking for any visible injuries.

"I'm fine. Where's Jason? What's going on?"

"Ameria's made the first move. She's finally attacking us." Alec's eyes fade before returning to look at me. "And Jason with currently with Aurelia, Kane and Rose. He's getting their forces ready. Is Ameria gets close to the heart of our Colony, then he's releasing them and himself as the final team."

"So we're hoping on the warriors to fend off the enemy?"

Alec smirks deviously. "They're my warriors. Beta trained. They're my best being released. Then we'll have the King release his best."

I bite my lip while I look around at all the warriors.

"Luna, we need to get you to safety," Alec says, taking me out of my thoughts.

I nod turning back to where Thomas sits in his wolf form. "Thomas, take me to Jason, I need to see him."

I turn my attention back to Alec and I grab his hand. "And you better be careful. You're my Beta too, you serve me. So listen to me when I say you better not die. I do not give that order, you are not allowed to do so."

I squeeze his hand and he squeezes back. "Yes, Luna."

I pull my hand away, turning back to Thomas. I don't look back as I walk beside Thomas, but I still here Alec give the final command and the tear of clothes to know they've shifted. To hear they're growls and snarls. It's only when it gets silent that I turn around a final time before entering the packhouse, to notice that Alec and his warriors are gone. Possibly forever.

"Jason!" My voice echoes through the packhouse. All the servants must have evacuated or have gone to a safe hold.

"Thomas, go change. I'm going to find Jason."

I run up the stairs and go to the only place I could think he would be right now.

I run down the hall, stopping when I meet five warriors outside his office. "Let me in."

The warriors do so without question, and the doors open to a busy filled office. Jason, Aurelia and Kane currently stare down at a map of the city while Rose sits at the side, staring off at a spot on the ground with her arms crossed.

"Jason."

Everyone in the room looks towards me, Jason's eyes widening.

"Thank the goddess, you're here."

He moves towards me embracing me and kissing me on the forehead.

His hands cup my cheeks as he inspects me. "Are you okay? I had some of my warriors go out to find you until Thomas mind linked me saying he was with you." Jason looks behind me, his eyebrows scrunching together. "Where is Thomas?"

"We split when we arrived while looking for you."

"Well, you're with me now." He turns back looking at Kane and Aurelia. "While Alec sent out the first wave of attacks, we've been planning and readying our combined forces. Thinking when to attack."

He moves towards the table and I join his side looking at the map. Indicators are placed where Ameria's forces have already attacked and where she is currently attacking.

"So far we've been able to hold our ground but we don't know what Ameria will pull out next. There hasn't been any sightings or reports through the mind link and-"

A gasp of pain comes out of Jason and he slightly sways on his feet.

The door opens and Thomas comes rushing in, a pained look on his face.

"You felt it too." He says as he walks in towards Jason.

I put my hands on Jason to help steady him. "What's wrong?"

Thomas grunts as he makes it to the table. "Jason has ties with every member in his pack. We all do, but the higher your title the bigger impact you feel. And when someone dies, he feels it, but when someone important to him or his pack gets badly injured or that member dies, the pain he feels is passed along to his important followers, like his guardians and beta and delta to let them know." Thomas looks up at Jason. "And someone important, close to Jason has just gotten severely injured."

Jason hisses in pain and his eyes fade and so do Thomas's. A minute later, they return and Jason's hands form to knuckles and he releases a low growl.

"Who is it?"

Jason ignores me, his eyes glowing, his voice deepening in anger. He turns to the Warriors in the room.

"I want him returned here now!"

Jason's eyes fade as he walks around, his claws extending.

"Jason," Thomas warns.

"I want some of the warriors bringing him back here right now."

"They'll do their best," Thomas explains.

Jason turns and in the blink of an eye, his hand is at his brother's throat.

"Jason, stop!" I yell.

At that moment I see another side of Jason. A side I haven't really seen before. He cares for his pack, his colony, the people deeply and he will do whatever it takes to save them.

A loud bang goes off in the distance and my head turns to the window to see a burst of fire and smoke release into the air off into the distance.

The town has been set ablaze. It's going to turn to ash and rubble.

I look down at the entrance gates from the window, only for my heart to skip a beat. There, injured at battered is Alec and a few of his men retreating.

My eyebrows scrunch together. Alec would never retreat unless he absolutely had to. I look off in distance and I suck in a breath.

"Jason, release the second wave of warriors now."

I hear multiple footsteps come up behind me and all of us stare out the window to see Ameria's warriors charging towards the packhouse.

CHAPTER 37: WAR

PART 3

Ameria's forces were long and stretched off into the distance. No wonder she had gotten so close. I starred out the window until I looked down at a familiar face. I couldn't break my stare, it's been too long since I've seen him. I thought he was dead, he should be dead.

I can hear everyone move away from the window, commands and orders being shouted behind me, but I don't break my stare. Not until he stops in the crowd and looks up at me in the eyes.

Those forest green eyes. Aiwin.

As soon as I make eye contact with him, the dagger sheath at my thigh seems to throb as if coming to life. I look down at my dagger to see the magic inside swirl awake.

I look back down to see Aiwin's eyes intense gaze still on me and I turn away as if feeling weak just by his stare.

Why hadn't Ameria killed him after she found out he betrayed her? Why would he still serve her afterwards?

I look back out the window to find him gone and a knot forms in my stomach.

Why is he—

"Luna,"

I turn away from the window, my questions being shoved aside as I turn to Thomas.

"We need to get you to safety."

I look to Rose who stands beside Kane, deep in thought, not even sparing me a glance. I then look to Aurelia who leans against the wall, her hooded cloak shielding her face. And then to Jason, the only one looking at me with a pained expression.

"I'm not going anywhere. I've run from Ameria, been afraid of her since the moment I got here."

"Good," Aurelia interrupts as she leans off the wall. She pulls down her hood so I can see her better. "You should be afraid of her."

I clench my hands into fists. "I'm not leaving."

Jason's nostrils flare. "Yes, you are. Ameria's forces will be here any second. I will be fighting along with the second wave of warriors and I do not want you to get caught in this fight. You've already had your battle with her. Aren't you tired of fighting?"

I can feel my anger rise like a volcano, ready to erupt but I take a calm breath. "What Ameria did to me only made me stronger. She made me kill people, put a weapon in my hands and gave me no choice but to shoot. She isolated me, made people laugh at me, hate me for who I was. I was trapped in a room full of darkness that I was sure should have consumed me. But here I am, still fighting. And I will never be done fighting until I see her kneeling before me."

Jason opens his mouth to say something but I cut him off. "I chose to put a weapon in my hands this time. This is my home now, our home. I am the Luna of this colony and I am not going to run and hide while I make others do the dirty work of saving it."

At that moment, the doors burst open and a wounded Alec comes limping in with the support of another warrior.

"Alec." Jason rushes over to Alec where he takes a seat in a chair.

His front abdomen is a bloody mess, and blood drips down the corner of his head.

Jason kneels in front of Alec, examining his wounds. "I'll have you sent down the safe passages out of here."

Alec looks up at Jason wide-eyed.

"But I'm your Beta. I'll fight with you until I die."

"Your time isn't today. I need you to rest up so you can protect your Luna with Thomas."

I shake my head. "Jason I already—"

A loud bang shakes the entire mansion and I fall my hands and knees.

Aurelia suddenly stands. "They're here."

Jason stumbles forward toward the table. "Call your forces forward."

Both Kane and Aurelia nod and Jason's eyes fog over as he mind links the rest of the Warriors.

Another bang shakes the house and I find myself struggling to get to my feet.

Multiple screams come from inside the house and I know that they must be coming inside now.

"Liz," Jason yells over the screams. "Take Alec and get to safety. Thomas will lead you."

I snarl but look over at Alec; bloody and defeated, ruined. He needs help and everyone will be busy protecting.

"Fine, but only because Alec needs help."

I move over to Alec, helping him up. A groan escapes his mouth as I help lifting him up.

"Lead the way, Thomas."

"Wait, Liz."

Jason makes a final move towards me and I turn away. "You may be the Alpha Jason but you will not control me. Never tell me what to do."

I put my hand on the doorknob until I hear him once again. "I'm sorry. Things will be different after, I promise."

I look up at Jason and my stomach twists, my heart aches. "Don't make promises you can't keep, Alpha."

And before he can say anything else, I open the door and I slam it shut behind me.

I follow Thomas through the hallways and I do my best to keep out the screams and cries. Alec puts most of his weight on me and I struggle at moments to keep my legs underneath me. Thomas leads on with a predatory look in his eyes, ready to run into any prey.

Maids and citizens run past us all with the same fear in their eyes. Picture frames have fallen off walls, glass crunches under my boots.

Thomas stops suddenly and turns to me. "Most of Ameria's warriors will be coming in through the easiest way. Jason had a secret exit built here and that's where I'm taking you. If what is true, then Ameria's men have already made their way inside and we'll most likely run into them. Stay close and stay behind me. Let me do the fighting."

I nod, gripping tighter on to Alec who holds onto conscious.

We pick up the pace, making our way to the secret passage when the window beside me crashes, the glass falling on top of me.

I move to cover Alec in the process, we go tumbling towards the ground and I lose hold of him. Glass falls around us and I put my hands over my head to protect myself. When I feel it's safe, I look up-glass falling off my head-towards Alec and Thomas. Alec shakily tries to get up onto his knees while up ahead, Thomas battles with some of Ameria's warriors who have just gotten inside.

He's half transformed, his wolf claws and speed taken over. Right as he slashes an enemy across the chest, he looks back at me for a split second before moving onto the next enemy and yelling back at me.

"Liz, get Alec up and trail back! He knows the way!"

Thomas cuts through the enemies, his Guardian role in protecting his Luna taking over. More enemies begin to pile in though and we're greatly outnumbered here.

I get up, noticing blood trail down my arms and knees from the glass. I ignore the sting on my skin and the feeling of blood trickling down. I help Alec up, a groan escaping his lips.

"Alec," His eyes droop slightly, blood stains his shirt, his skin is awfully pale.

I wrap my arm around his waist, and I grip his hand which hangs over my neck. I look over at Thomas who looks back at me for a split second. Blood drips from his claws but I don't miss the nod he gives me.

Ignoring my wanting to help stay and fight with him, I trail back like he said for Alec's sake. He's the Beta, he needs to survive too.

We make our way through the halls blindly. I have no clue where I'm going.

"Alec," I shake him slightly but he stays quiet.

When we get farther from where the fighting is happening, I sit him down carefully.

"Alec," I whisper. His eyes stay closed and I continue to shake him. "Alec," I repeat and a groan escapes his lips.

A breath of relief escapes me and I place my hands on his shoulders to get his attention on me. "Alec," I say finally and he focuses on me.

"Liz?"

"Alec I need your help. Where is the secret passage? In order for me to help you, you need to help me."

He shuts his eyes for a second as he tries to remember. "We need to get to the other side of the house. From there—"

Alec suddenly stops, eyes squinting. "We're not alone."

He struggles to get up, gripping his bloody side, but he still manages to get up and stand in front me when a man turns the corner and stands on the opposite end of the hallway.

Alec growls, the dagger at my side throbs to life and that alone tells me who it is.

"Looking good, Elizabeth. It's been a while."

I pull my dagger out, moving beside Alec so I can get a better view of him.

Aiwin.

CHAPTER 38. FOLLOW

Aiwin stands there in his black uniform, a crossbow hanging across his back, daggers sheathed against his thighs, arrows strapped along his back.

The dagger he gave me throbs in my hand, faster and faster as if Aiwin is making it come to life.

Alec sways on his feet beside me, but nonetheless holds his ground to protect me.

"Aiwin, leave us be. I'm just trying to get Alec to safety so I can take care of his wounds."

"I see. Someone isn't feeling the best."

Blood drops onto the floor from Alec's wounds, his skin tone is pale, sweat forms on his forehead.

"Alec?"

Alec sways on his feet and his eyes flutter close. He falls to the floor and I reach out to grab him.

"Alec!"

He collapses to the floor, taking me with him.

I can see Aiwin take a step closer but I aim my dagger towards him.

"Stay back!"

Aiwin stops, a crease forming in his forehead as he thinks.

I turn my focus to Alec, his pale figure.

"Alec."

He's dying."

I turn to Aiwin, my dagger pointed towards him. "Shut up."

Aiwin takes a step towards me but I raise the dagger even higher, giving him a side glance.

"Don't think I won't do it. I will."

Aiwin raises his hands defensively. "I don't doubt your abilities at all. You proved that to me in Ameria's mansion."

I snarl at the memory. At the blood on my hands, shaking as I stared at them

"Leave me. I need to tend to his wounds before it's too late."

"I see that. I can hear his heart slowing."

I look down at Alec and then to Aiwin, shaking my head. "Hear his heart?-Who—What are you?"

"He's not going to make it, Elizabeth. Your Beta is as good as dead, I'm sorry."

I look down at Alec's unconscious, sweaty figure. His breathing is ragged, his skin pale.

I feel myself come on the verge of tears as I crouch down to Alec and put my hand on his cheek.

"I'm not here to hurt you, Liz. I'm here to save you."

I move to hold Alec's hand, his cold, limp hand. "Alec," I whisper, shaking him slightly. "Alec," I say more forceful.

"Liz—"

I turn to Aiwin, tears forming in my eyes. "Leave me alone!"

I turn back to Alec and I know he's gone. I know. I look down at my bloodstained hands, his blood.

A cry escapes my mouth and I hug Alec's lifeless body. I may not be connected to the mind link, but I know they felt it. The howls in the distance prove that.

They howl when they lose a loved one or someone of importance: that's what I read in the library a while back again.

"It's okay, it's okay." I rock back in fourth slightly while hugging Alec.

Liz, Ameria's forces are winning. She will find you and she will kill you once she takes over Wolf Colony and your mate won't be able to save you while he's held captive. I'm not here to give you to her, I'm here to save you."

I focus on Alec's face, the Beta to the King, the Queen: me. I put my hand to his cheek. "You have served your Colony well. Rest peacefully."

The house suddenly shakes slightly, the sound of screams getting louder.

"Liz." Aiwin presses. "Please, I can get you out of here, now is the time. Ameria thinks I'm capturing you right now."

I stand silently, turning to Aiwin with anger. "You did this." I spit.

Aiwin stands straight, looking me in the eyes. "No, Ameria did.

I'm here to try and save Wolf Colony."

"What?"

"Liz, listen to me. Ameria will take over Wolf Colony. Jason will be held captive or be forced to rule by her side."

"What about me?"

Aiwin gives me a sad look. "Dead. She has no use for you. But if I can get you out, disappear, I can help you."

"How?" I press.

The house shakes more aggressively again and Aiwin takes his crossbow in his hands. "You are the Colonies only hope. If Ameria takes over, I can get you away, help you build your own army and you can take back what's yours."

I stand there, more confused than ever. "I thought you serve Ameria."

"I did. Until I saw you and felt . . . something pulls me towards you. That's why I helped you escape and now that I'm here with you again, away from Ameria's grasp, I can help you escape and live."

I take a step back. "Aiwin I—"

Aiwin moves closer to me. "Listen to me, if you don't leave then you will die. Is that what you want? Please, just listen to me. Either die today or live to fight back another."

I look down at Alec's lifeless body. That could be me. I look up at Aiwin, this man who wants to help me because of some pull. But what other options do I have? I'm running out of time.

I look up at Aiwin, the urgency and slight panic in his eyes. But what stands out is his urgency to help me, save me. He's telling the truth.

I look Aiwin in the eyes and I grip my dagger even tighter. "Get me out of here."

Aiwin nods but right as he turns I grab his sleeve, pointing the dagger at him. "I hope you know that I am leaving everything behind. So you better not be playing me for some fool because believe me when I say I will not hesitate to hurt you if you hurt me."

A small smirk forms on Aiwin's face replacing the slight panic that was in his eyes earlier. "I'd rather not get on that side of your's anyway."

I nod, pointing a hand in front of me to let him lead. I sheath my dagger and I follow.

CHAPTER 39: PROTECTOR

I follow Aiwin through the packhouse, trusting in him that he will get me to safety. Yes, he has told me why I should trust him but I still always keep my hand on my dagger to make sure that if he does betray me, I will be ready.

"We need to jump out a window to leave," Aiwin says looking back at me. "Is that alright?"

I nod, when suddenly one of Ameria's Warriors turn a corner, facing us.

My eyes widen and I'm about to warn Aiwin when he turns quickly, raising his crossbow and firing an arrow into the creature's heart.

It goes down with a thud and low growl of pain. From where I stand, blood oozes from the wound and I grimace, the memory of Alec's body coming to mind.

The sound of growling and footsteps knocks me out of my thoughts when a group of Ameria's warriors turn the corner, staring down at the dead creature.

Aiwin whistles, grabbing their attention to him.

"Are you stupid?" I yell as the creatures advance on to him.

Aiwin smiles, his eyes full of excitement as if he's been waiting for this moment.

I stand slightly behind Aiwin, feeling my heart pound against my chest as I stare at the creatures.

They move towards us and Aiwin holds his ground while my move back slightly.

Aiwin." I warn.

His smile grows, the creatures get closer.

"Aiwin," I repeat.

And closer.

Aiwin looks into his aiming scope.

Closer.

"Aiwin!"

He fires, the arrow soars, and he reloads as that arrow finds its home in the closest creatures chest.

Aiwin continues to fire at them until they're all dead on the ground, a pool of blackish blood staining the floor.

I look down at my own hands. Alec's blood.

I feel tears gather in my eyes, my throat and chest tightening.

"Liz."

I look up at Aiwin, I didn't realize he had gotten so close.

He looks down at my hands and then back at my face.

"We need to keep moving." He says quieter, gently.

I nod as I'm on the verge of tears, speaking would make me break.

I continue to follow Aiwin, staying silent the whole time.

We arrive outside a cracked window, two stories up and Aiwin opens it.

He leans against the ledge, looking up and down, making sure it is clear. He then saddles the window ledge before looking at me and nodding.

I already know what I'll have to do. Holding back my slight fear, I push it down and I straddle the window, facing Aiwin. I look at him for a split second before bringing my leg over and jumping off. I fall, rolling upon contact with the ground. When I get up onto my feet, I turn when I hear a thud to see Aiwin standing behind me, crossbow back in his hands.

The sounds of fighting are not too far, no doubt we will get caught during our escape.

"Follow me and stay close."

I stay silent, but nod and continue to follow.

We run along the side of the packhouse as quickly as we can, but when we turn the corner, it's absolute chaos.

Everywhere I look is red. The side of the pack house stone is stained red now, blood stains the grass.

Countless fights take place. The sound of screams, skin breaking and blooding splattering against the ground fill the air.

I'm too shocked to move as I watch a werewolf jump on one of Ameria's creatures, ripping its head clean off with its teeth. Another fight, the creature swipes it's talons against a person's chest, blood splattering on the ground.

I hear Aiwin calling my name but its muffled as I continue to stare at the countless fights taking place.

Ameria is winning, we're outnumbered.

Where are Jason and Rose?

I hear my name called again and I turn to Aiwin whose hands are clenching the sleeves of my shoulders, shaking me slightly.

My name sounds muffled but slowly clears as Aiwin repeats my name and I shake my head, everything speeding up again.

"Elizabeth!"

I grab onto Aiwins arms myself, showing him I'm okay.

"We need to get out of here! Follow me!"

We run through the chaos, dodging attacks, the swipes of claws and blood splatters. It would be impossible to come out clean. I can already feel the blood on my shirt sticking to my skin.

As I run, I scan the battlefield, searching for Jason, Rose, any familiar face. I can't just leave them behind, not when they've all given me so much.

I stop, digging my heels into the ground before screaming at the top of my lungs over the noise of war.

"Rose! Jason! Thomas!"

The chaos doesn't stop, no response is yelled back and I run my hands through my hair feeling panic rise in my chest.

"Elizabeth!"

I turn to find Aiwin coming towards me, no doubt realizing I wasn't behind him anymore. But he raises his crossbow at me and I take a step back, looking back and forth between the crossbow and Aiwin.

My panic is soon replaced by fear and betrayal. So this is what it's like to be hunted, to be on the other side, the one not pulling the trigger.

I find myself bracing myself, waiting for him to make that move, but instead, he screams one word at me before aiming.

Duck.

It takes me a second to register what he said before my eyes widen and I duck, my arms flying up to my face as I hear the arrow fly past above me. I turn on my knees, looking past me to see a creature charging towards me, only for arrows to be continuously shot into its chest. Aiwin makes his way beside me, continuing to aim and fire as he does so. He nudges me with his leg into my side and I get up, moving slightly behind him when someone pulls on the back on my neck collar, dragging me back.

I try reaching out and gripping Aiwin, but the creature pulls me hard, whipping me back and letting me land onto the ground hard. The back of my head hits the ground, the breath gets knocked out of me and I struggle back onto my feet, turning quickly to try and run away only to feel sharp talons meet the skin on my back, ripping and tearing at my skin. My scream pierces the air as I fall to the ground, my blood spreading around me.

A groan escapes me as I feel my hot blood drip down my back. I don't even make an effort to move, the pain in my back excruciating. I grip the grass into my hands attempting to crawl. I need to get out of here.

I feel a hand touch my shoulder and I scream, not in pain but out of fear. They turn me over and I kick and squirm, ready to fight with whatever I have left.

"Elizabeth, it's me!"

Aiwin, bloody and bruised coming to help me. I've never felt so relieved to see a familiar face.

"Aiwin," I breathe.

Aiwin looks me over and shakes his head once. "Let's get you out of here."

Before I know it, Aiwin helps me up, an arm around my waist supporting me up. "Can you walk?"

My breathing is ragged, my back hurts to the point where it's numb, the world slightly spins around me, but I nod. "Yes, I can walk," I say as I pull out my dagger.

I follow Aiwin through the mass of bodies fighting, the wolves jumping and prowling, the blood splattering against skin and fur.

We make it to the edge of the fight, close to the tree line with still no sign of Rose, Jason, Thomas, or anyone we'd recognize.

"Aiwin—"

"They're okay. Come back here, the trees will hide us."

I rub the crease forming in my forehead and I blink away the tears forming. They're okay, they have to be.

I follow Aiwin into the forest, escaping the disaster that has taken place, away from Ameria.

We stop at a small clearing and I collapse onto the dirt.

"We'll stop for now. If anyone made it out, they'll come here."

I look down at my bloodied hands, at my blood stained clothes and I feel the bile rise up in my throat. I double over, heaving up any food that was left in me. I feel my hair get tied back gently as I empty my stomach.

Who's blood is this?

"I had to get you out," Aiwin says softly as I settle down. "You're the Queen and Ameria would have killed you."

I sit back on my heels slowly, wiping my mouth with the back of my wrist. "What about Jason, he's the King of Alphas."

"If he made it out, they would be headed in this direction. And Ameria won't kill him, she wants a King for herself to rule. You'd just get in the way."

I look back in the direction we came from. "It's gotten quiet."

Aiwin nods before looking up at the sky. The sun has almost set, the night is to come. "The fight is almost over. Ameria has taken control."

"Won't she be looking for you?"

"No, I severed my ties to her at the right moment so she couldn't follow me. I just needed the right time."

"She saw you betray her right in front of her eyes. How are you still alive?"

"I'm one of her most trusted warriors, a Shadow Warrior to be exact and there are laws, bonds and she can't just kill me. However, she believed Aurelia put some spell on me to force me to do what I did."

"Why would you stand alongside her?"

Aiwin up looks at the evening sky before looking down at me. "There's a lot you don't know about me."

"Looks like we've got time."

"I'm a Fae Prince, a warrior, protector. Ameria was going to take over my Colony—or back then, it was my parents'. But they offered a deal, take two Fae princes as her Shadows: the best warriors she could ever have. Our skill set, discipline, and fighting skills make us one of the most experienced warriors in this world. So long as she would leave us alone, she would receive more Shadows so she could take over other colonies with the aid of Fae Colony."

I exhale. "You're a Fae prince?"

Aiwin nods. "America's ultimate army will be made up of Shadows. She will take over the whole world. I believed it too until I saw you."

I raise an eyebrow. "Me?"

"Fae's have bonds too, Elizabeth. More sacred and powerful than a wolfs. When we find our bonds, we become protectors, bodyguards to that person. We'll love them and protect them to our last breath, loyal to our dying day."

I take a step back. "What are you saying?"

Aiwin stands, setting his shoulders back. "You're my bond. I'm your protector."

CHAPTER 40: FALLEN QUEEN

It's moments like these where your heart feels like it stops.
"What?"

The only words that stick in my mind are Prince, Protector, bond.

"I can't have a bond with you Aiwin. I'm Jason's mate."

Aiwin smiles slightly. "I don't have to be your mate Elizabeth. Fae's bonds work differently, I can be whoever you wish me to be. Unlike your bond with Jason's, it's set romantically."

I sit on the ground, taking this all in.

"But I am your protector, Liz." Aiwin continues. "It is my job to make sure you don't get hurt."

"Your job," I repeat before a scream and a cry comes in the direction of the packhouse.

I get up, moving in that direction again when Aiwin grabs my wrist.

"You can't, you'll be seen, the forest isn't as thick on the edge."

I raise an eyebrow, yanking my wrist out of his grasp. "*My people are in trouble. A prince like you should understand.*"

Another scream echoes through the forest. The hairs on the back of my neck stand up and I move forward again only for Aiwin to grab me, desperation evident in his eyes. "Ameria will kill you if she sees you."

"I just need to see."

Another scream pierces the air followed by cries.

I move forward, ignoring Aiwins' protests. I pass through the thick of the trees, following the screams and the cries.

As they get louder, closer, I crouch down, moving closer and closer.

Through the thick of the trees, I can make out the packhouse and Ameria's creatures surrounding the area.

Bodies lay on the ground, inhuman and wolf form and I feel tears form.

Those are my people.

Those *were* my people.

My heart and chest ache, I feel a need to reach out. To do *something*

"Liz," Aiwin whispers. "You don't want to see this."

I ignore Aiwin and I move slightly closer noticing kneeling figures.

"Who . . ." I drift off as I try to make out the group of people.

"Liz, please."

My eyes widen, and I fall back on my heels.

My friends: Rose, Thomas, Jason. Even Aurelia and Kane kneel alongside them.

Aurelia stands in front of them, with creatures beside her.

She speaks to them, but they keep their heads down, silent.

What's happening?" I ask Aiwin, but he stays silent.

"Aiwin," I demand.

Ameria points to Thomas suddenly and the creatures pick him up forcefully by each arm. Jason stands, interfering, trying to help his brother. I look around the area hastily, trying to find something, anything that could help, so I could do something.

More of Ameria's creatures hold Jason down and for a moment, Ameria stops, looking like she's deciding something, calculating.

The palms of my hands become clammy, my mouth dry.

Ameria's creatures suddenly bring Jason forward instead and hold Thomas.

My heart skips a beat, pounds against my chest.

Ameria slaps him across the face and I inch forward, my jaw and hands clenching my whole body tense.

Thomas thrashes forward against his grip with the creatures, trying to free himself.

"What's going on?" I whisper.

I turn to Aiwin, but he only responds with silence.

I then turn back to the scene to see Ameria's creatures force Jason down to his knees.

She stares down at him as if the sight is liberating to her. But he doesn't look at her, instead, as if he can feel my presence nearby, he looks towards the trees, in my direction.

My heart clenches, I want to reach out to him. I know he's looking straight at me, I know he can see me.

But then Ameria's creature raises its talon, claws extended and all.

No.

I'm about to scream out, to yell, to step forward and stop.

But I notice the slight shake of Jason's head, his peaceful smile.

And then the creature brings down its claw, cleaning Jason's head right off.

My mouth is opened in a silent scream and shock. Perhaps I really was screaming when Aiwin grabs me, embraces me so I'm no longer looking and muffles my cries and screams.

My mate. Dead.

Gone.

I shake my head, tears staining my cheeks and Aiwins' clothes and gear.

"They killed him," I mumble against Aiwin. "They killed him."

The ache in my chest, in my heart. I feel like I can't move like my limbs are frozen in time. As if my mind can't comprehend what happened.

Ameria took him away from me as everyone else I love.

I'm alone.

I know at some point, Aiwin helps lead us farther into the depth of the forest. I don't know how far away we travelled, but Aiwin never lets me go. The only time he did was when he believed we were safe and placed me down gently.

My throats feels raw from crying, my cheeks are tear-stained, my eyes feel puffy. My clothes are still stained red, so are my hands and arms and torn at my back from getting slashed.

"Aiwin," I speak weakly as he sets me down, inspecting me.

"Turn around. Let me see your back." He says softly but sternly.

"It's dark out, you won't be able to see. And I'm tired. I'm not feeling the best."

I go to lay down but Aiwin holds onto my shoulders, looking into my eyes. "Let me help." He slightly smiles when I don't protest and moves around me to view my back. I can hear his sharp intake of breath but I ignore it.

"You've lost a lot of blood and you're dehydrated. I need to clean this wound before it gets infected."

I block out what he says, not caring, but thinking. Where do I go from here? What if America killed everyone else?

Aiwin moves back in front of me, holding my shoulders. He opens a pouch at his waist pulling out a small white pill.

"Take this."

He places it in the palm of my hand, waiting.

"What is it?"

"It'll help lessen the pain."

I take it while Aiwin moves to face my back again.

He dabs my back with a piece of cloth and the smell antiseptic fills the air.

My back stings . . . a lot and I bite my lip to stay silent.

"You really took a beating, Liz."

I look up at the treetops, the night sky shining down. "They're all dead, aren't they?"

Aiwin stops moving for a second before resuming as if contemplating the best response to tell a wounded soldier. "No, I think *some* of them are still alive. I doubt Ameria would kill them all in one sitting. That's not her style."

"I don't know if that's better or not." I hiss in pain as Aiwin dabs a sensitive spot.

"We need to find a creek or river. Something to get this wound fully cleaned."

I nod, feeling my eyelids get heavy from the day.

My mate is dead.

I feel tears build up, my chest tightens and I feel hot tears spill down my cheeks. I continue to keep my back towards Aiwin so he doesn't notice, but I feel my shoulders shake and gentle hand on my shoulder tells me otherwise.

Before I know it, I'm bursting into a puddle of tears and my heartache takes over the pain in my back.

"My mate is dead. Jason is gone," I admit.

"I know," Aiwin states softly but I jump to my feet, turning on him.

"He's dead! You didn't let me do anything! You didn't do anything! He was the King!"

I can tell Aiwin doesn't know what to say or react. Or perhaps he's letting me speak my mind after everything that happened. But I didn't care. It was both our faults that people died today. And I failed.

I give up on the yelling and I continue to cry, falling to my knees like the fallen Queen I am.

CHAPTER 41. NEW PATHS

Every time I close my eyes, I remember the faces of those I've lost. I'm not surprised I didn't find sleep.

Trying to sleep on the forest floor wasn't fun, especially with my back torn up.

Aiwin helps me up gently as soon as the sun rays struck through the trees indicating it's time to set off.

"We need to find a source of water for you."

My throat is dry and scratchy as I speak. "And for you."

Aiwin smiles slightly. "My Fae body can last longer than a human body. You're my number one priority."

I stand up, wincing in pain as we move forward leaving everything behind us.

The hollow pit in my chest is still as horrible as ever.

I look over my shoulder in the direction of the packhouse, at all the people and memories I'll have to leave behind. If we don't move, Ameria will find us and we'll be dead. We have no choice.

"Liz?"

Aiwin snaps me out of my thoughts; a Fae prince, my protector.

"Let's go."

We trek onward as the sun rises wasting no time. Aiwin uses his senses as a guide, trying to hear, smell or see any water sources. From what he told me, Fae has heightened senses so in about an hour, we find a river that we drink from to replenish. Aiwin uses it to clean my wound which appears to not be healing as good as he thought.

"Where do we go from here? What's the plan?"

Aiwin leans back, looking up at the sky. I remember his brown hair almost looking black in Ameria's mansion, but out here in the sun, his hair is like a chestnut brown and his green eyes remind me of a forest—a complete opposite of Jason with his black and blue eyes—while Jason was a sharp and striking kind of handsome, Aiwin's seems more gentle—striking, his looks could definitely kill if needed but there seems to be a softer side that he'd hate to show.

"Liz, did you not hear a word I just said or are you too busy staring at me?"

I snap my eyes away, heat rising to my face and I turn away. "Sorry, something behind you grabbed my attention."

There's a moment of silence and I mentally urge him to talk. "Right. Well, Wolf Colony isn't safe for both of us, our safest solution would be to go to Fae colony, my home."

I turn around so quickly my heart stops. "Fae Colony? As in leave Wolf Colony and leave everyone that needs our help? These are my people, I can't just leave."

Aiwin stands, looking like he wants to reach out to me with his hands but refrains himself from doing so. "Do you think you can help your people with a bow and arrow against hundreds of Ameria's creatures and her magic?"

I open my mouth to say something but nothing comes out.

"We need help, Liz. And it's okay to ask for it. My people can lend some warriors, they can train you to fight."

"My friends need me."

"You injured and tired isn't going to help them."

I shake my head. "I don't want to leave them."

"You're not leaving them, Liz. You gathering your army, planning your attack will help them and save them. One thing I learned in my training was that if you want to win your wars you need to have patience. You can't just rush into battle."

"I want to help them now."

"Well, you can't Liz!" Aiwin breaks, an emotion other than bravery and part smart-ass breaking through. "Sometimes people need to realize that you can't help today and that you'll need to wait until tomorrow. You may want to, but you just can't. You don't have the people or army unless your prepared to do nothing for anyone and die. So until then, gather your people, make yourself strong, unstoppable, become a force to be reckoned with. Do you want to help your people? Good. But you need to be patient."

I stand there, fists clenching and unclenching as I turn and stare at the water rushing downstream.

I want to yell, scream at Aiwin, maybe even slap him. But what would that prove?

I look over my shoulder slightly towards Aiwin when my breathing evens out. "I'm not strong. How can I bring that image forward when I don't believe in what or who I am." I turn back toward the water, focusing on its current. "You tell me to be these things, but I'm not. Jason was strong, Rose was unstoppable, Thomas and Alec were fearless. They were an unstoppable force. Not me."

There's silence that follows until I hear Aiwin stand beside me. "And you are smart, daring, and brave. Maybe not so much physically strong," I laugh as Aiwin nudges my arm. "But mentally, you are."

I raise an eyebrow, furthering him to continue.

Who survived being in Ameria's grasp for a month? Surrounded by darkness and loneliness. Who had to survive and battle her nightmares alone? Real and fake? You did. And you continue to do so."

"That's because I had no choice. I had to be strong, I had to make it out of there. Not for me, but for Rose and Thomas and-and Jason."

The feel of tears come forth and I shut my eyes and calm my breathing. When I feel ready, I open them and start again. "I was strong for them. I wasn't going to just give up, I have a role to fulfil and I couldn't give up on that and just leave them."

I look back at the river and in the forest. "I want to be strong, I want to be like you. Fearless, determined, cunning, brave. I want to learn how to fight. Properly."

Aiwin crosses his arms over his chest. "You can. I can teach you. I can make you into a Fae warrior—a shadow—if that is what you want."

"A shadow Queen," I mumble.

"A Queen of Night, ruler of the Wolves." Aiwin repeats.

I then face Aiwin. "If that is what it takes to help my people. I want Ameria to pay and I want her to feel every bit of pain she has inflicted on me."

"Then let's go to Fae colony. Let's go so we can save your people."

I look at Aiwin, at his confidence, his muscles, his bravery. Yes, that is what I want to become. A fighter, a shadow whose eyes glow like a wolfs, who can fight like an assassin and stand up to her nightmares. No more hiding, no more being scared.

Ameria will pay and I will take Wolf Colony back.

Not just for me but for Rose, Thomas, Alec, and Jason. That was our home and she's messing with the wrong people.

"Let's go."

King of Alphas

ACKNOWLEDGEMENTS

This story was not meant to get out into the world, but here it is! This was a small project I did, and I had no intentions of publishing.

I want to thank many people so here it goes:

A special thanks to FicFun for publishing and advertising on their site. When you wanted to sign me on I thought I was dreaming.

To Wattpad, this platform is what helped this story become noticed. Without the help of many readers and authors, I would not be here today.

A thank you to Amazon and Kindle for helping this story come to life by giving me the tools I need to make this become a reality.

To my grandfather, as he always called me his firecracker, I hope you are proud of me.

A warm thank you to my family, especially my brother for working with me to help enhance my writing skills.

While writing this was no easy task, I want to thank all those who stuck by my side and continuously gave me words of encouragement to continue. You never gave up on me and I think that's why I never gave up on myself.

To the readers, if you made it this far, thank you! I am a young author and still have much to learn. You are the reason I get to where I want to be everyday. I hope to give you many more stories that not only get better but achieve so much more.

Made in the USA
Middletown, DE
16 February 2019